THE INTERGALACTIC INTERLOPER

THE INTERGALACTIC INTERLOPER

A NOVEL

DELAS HERAS

DOUBLE SIX BOOKS | NEW YORK

DOUBLE SIX BOOKS
www.doublesixbooks.com

The Intergalactic Interloper is a work of fiction.
Names, places, and characters are all products of the author's imagination.
Any resemblance to actual locales, persons, or events, is entirely coincidental.

ISBN 978-1-7353175-1-9 (pbk)
ISBN 978-1-7353175-0-2 (ebook)

To Nicole, who made this book possible

O. AXZLEPROVA

[three weeks earlier]

The barrel-shaped vessel glided down from the sky, landing light as a feather on the silvery rooftop of an unexceptional East Village building. Nine stories tall, the apartment building ran the length of the block between Fourth and Fifth Streets. Seen from above, it looked like a chunky letter E.

The night was moonless and overcast, and a sudden neighborhood blackout ensured the extraordinary arrival went unnoticed by any local night owls.

Minutes later, when the lights came back on, the roof appeared the same as it always had. Only instead of one water tower, there were now two. Both exactly alike: made of weathered steel with long spindly legs and a narrow ladder welded along the side, leading up to a cone-shaped roof.

The southernmost tower, in the center of the roof, was the new addition. Inside this tower there was a circular cabin packed with a rather impressive array of sophisticated controls, built around a sleek command chair. Alien invasion movie buffs would have approved of the creature nestled in this sleek chair, as it was not unlike the projected imaginings of their favorite silver screen flicks: It was a bipedal tortoise-like animal with a large round body and two oval heads poking out on sinewy necks from a shell. Each head had two forward-facing heavily lidded eyes, a lipless mouth, and two long antennae protruding from bald skulls. It had four arms—two on each side of its huge shell—each arm ending in an eight-fingered hand, for a grand total of thirty-two digits.

Its scaly skin was a dappled chartreuse, but it had the ability to change its color to match the surroundings, including its shell, so that when it emerged from the ship its only discernible features were its four yellow eyes, seemingly floating in thin air. And when its eyelids slid shut it became utterly invisible.

Even so, this extraplanetary visitor was cautious, venturing out only at night, keeping to the shadows, and always worried that the gamble it had made, by parking in plain sight, might prove to be a costly mistake.

1. OLLIE

[7 a.m., October 13, 1995]

Ollie and his cat, Pirate, lived in a dreary walk-up on East Fourth Street. It was a pretty enough red brick building as seen from the street—six stories tall, with narrow windows set in rows of eight and a fire escape that zigzagged down the facade. But inside it was all ramshackle apartments with low ceilings and crumbling walls.

His tiny studio was on the top floor in the back, a space with a worrisome lack of right angles where walls, floor, and ceiling met. Ollie guessed that the building must have settled strangely, throwing the architect's best efforts completely out of whack. The floor was so heavily tilted, and the apartment such a postage stamp, that Ollie could easily slide on his socks from one end to the other—so long as he was traveling down hill.

His apartment was sparsely furnished: a twin-size bed, a futon couch, a beat-up coffee table he'd found on the street, and a desk that held a boxy television set and a record player. The walls were bare except for a Yellow Submarine poster pinned above the couch and a plain rectangular mirror hanging on the wall by the front door. He'd hung this mirror from a fat nail that had made an alarming web of cracks in the plaster as he hammered it in. He had balanced the mirror carefully on the nail and then stepped back, holding his breath. Nothing happened. The mirror hung there, dutifully, for the next ten months. Then, at the crack of dawn one October morning, it came crashing down, jolting him awake.

He leaped out of bed in a panic and stood there, frozen. Ollie was tall and lanky, with a mop of unruly black hair. He snatched his glasses from the nearby desk and dropped the square black frames in place over his light blue eyes. His world came into focus. His gaze followed the trail of scattered glass back to the smashed-up mirror on the floor, and from there to the small crater in the wall where the nail had been. Then he looked around anxiously for Pirate, but his cat was nowhere to be seen.

Barefoot, he picked his way carefully past shards of glass, retrieved a dustpan and brush from the closet, and set about sweeping up the mess. Ollie considered himself only moderately superstitious. He wasn't the kind of person who went into a panic over spilled salt. Still, a broken mirror first thing in the morning gave him pause.

He disposed of the fragments, ran the vacuum, brushed his teeth, and pulled on his usual white T-shirt and blue jeans. A black leather jacket, hanging on a hook by the door, completed his simple look, which was inspired by the album covers and posters of his punk idols. But instead of heading out to work, he began to pace back and forth in his socks. He was worried about Pirate. There was no sign of that cat anywhere, and his food bowl from last night was untouched. Ollie had installed a pet flap in his fire escape window and Pirate had gone off yesterday for his usual evening ramble. His regular route led him down the fire escape to the third floor, where he would slip through the bars onto a tree branch. From there he could wind up just about anywhere in the neglected courtyards below. Ollie took a peek out the window, but his view was mostly blocked by a mass of dense yellow leaves. He shook his head glumly—autumn was a melancholy time of year to begin with, but if you added missing cats to the equation, things quickly became hopeless.

He had first set eyes on Pirate a little over a year ago when the tomcat materialized on his fire escape on a stormy September morning. The bedraggled animal had gotten himself caught outside in a downpour, and Ollie, taking pity on him, had opened his window and let him inside. Pirate quickly took a liking to the place, and they'd been roommates ever since. Ollie was new in town back then, and he'd been struggling to adjust to the hard edges of city life. But once Pirate appeared in his life, everything had magically clicked into place.

He knew that cats sometimes went missing for days without anyone kicking up a fuss, and that they often turned up again later, no worse for the wear. But he had a bad feeling that his whiskered friend was in trouble. Ollie, who was still pacing back and forth, spinning on his heels every time he hit a wall, was stopped in his tracks by a sharp knock on his door. Putting his eye to the peephole, Ollie groaned when he recognized his downstairs neighbor Constance Frizzler.

She was a trim woman in her thirties, with grubby hair and beady eyes, who worked as a court stenographer. She liked to wander the building's hallways and stairs in a pink bathrobe while talking to herself. A robe she was currently wearing.

He grudgingly opened the door. "Hello, Constance."

"What the hell are you doing smashing things at the crack of dawn? You nearly gave me a heart attack!" she snapped, glaring at him.

"I'm very sorry—my mirror fell off the wall this morning. Completely accidental."

"And what's with all the stomping around?"

"I was just pacing in my socks—it can't have been very loud."

"Easy for you to say. I live downstairs and I can tell you that it sounds like an elephant is clomping back and forth on my ceiling."

Ollie sincerely doubted this. He didn't recall any clomping. He wasn't sure clomping was even feasible in socks. Constance was just overly sensitive. She frequently trekked up the stairs to bang on his door when he was playing his steel-string acoustic. He suspected her complaints had very little to do with actual noise levels. It was the mere thought of a musician living overhead that drove her crazy.

Still, he did his best to defuse the situation. "I'm sorry. I'm just worried about my cat. He's gone missing. And when I get worried I pace."

"That fat cat of yours who likes to climb the tree in the courtyard?" Her eyes narrowed. Ollie nodded, and Constance sniffed. "For the life of me I can't see why you let that wretched animal roam all over the neighborhood."

Ollie cleared his throat. "You haven't seen him anywhere, have you?"

"I see him all the time. He always seems to be prowling around my fire escape."

"But have you seen him recently?" he persisted.

"I'm afraid not," she said, managing to sound not the least bit sorry. "How long has he been gone?"

"Since about sundown last night. He missed his midnight dinner, and breakfast, too, which isn't like him at all. You can always count on him to be front and center come feeding time."

"I can tell he's a good eater just by looking at him," she said. "That cat of yours probably snapped a branch of that poor tree." Constance's eyebrows knit together once more. "Well if he does turn up, do me a favor and keep him away from my windows. He scares my bunnies something awful. Of course I never let *my* girls roam around outside. That's a bad idea." Constance kept three rabbits in the apartment below, which Ollie suspected was quite a lot of rabbits for a small studio the same size as his own.

"Well cats aren't really like bunnies though, are they?" he pointed out defensively.

"Well cats are not like squirrels either," she snarled. "They shouldn't be climbing trees!" And with that parting remark she stormed back down the stairs.

Ollie shook his head and muttered something unintelligible under his breath. Back home neighbors were neighborly. They did things like bake you apple pies, and dress appropriately. Here your downstairs neighbor was practically a mortal enemy.

2. ZARA

[7:30 a.m.]

Zara was sitting on a two-tone orange bench in the foremost car of an F train that was rattling along a dark tunnel somewhere below Queens. Sitting on the bench opposite her was a grim-faced man wearing a dingy jean jacket. He had graying hair, a wiry beard, and was staring right at her with his one good eye, the other being hidden behind an eyepatch. Or perhaps he was staring through her? It was hard to tell, but either way it was unnerving. He looked like he could step into the role of villain on any Hollywood film set—no questions asked. Zara buried her nose a little further in her book on Exotic Animal Medicine, but in actuality her thoughts were focused on willing an invisible protective bubble around herself.

She was often ill at ease on the subway, so unlike her familiar Underground back home. The Tube was cleaner, it didn't smell quite so revolting, and people were generally more polite—as in not staring. Here in New York you needed something called a "subway face." She was still working on hers. But she'd mastered the trick of scurrying over to the neighboring car to get away from any creeps. A move she might soon need to implement to get away from eyepatch man's cyclopean glare.

It took about forty-five minutes to get from Forest Hills to Fourteenth Street at Sixth Avenue, and from there it was a ten-minute walk to the veterinary hospital. She was doing clinical rotations in New York for a year, and moving in with her Aunt Zelda in Forest Hills had seemed like the perfect plan. But she hadn't realized that she would be setting her alarm for before first light every day.

Zara had come to New York to put some much-needed distance between herself and her cheating bastard of an ex-boyfriend. What a fool she'd been. Six months had passed since their breakup and she was still gutted. She would never forget the moment her whole world suddenly turned inside out. The day she'd realized it had been nothing but lies from day one.

The train swayed back and forth as it hurtled along. The text in her book was suddenly blurred. Zara blinked up at the fluorescent tube lights. *God help me. The last thing I need is to burst into tears with eyepatch guy's one eye locked on me.* Taking a deep breath, Zara pushed her tangled thoughts of London betrayals from her mind. She glanced at her watch and was relieved to discover she was more or less on time. She had a long day ahead of her, but at least it was Friday, which meant she would be meeting the boys later for a Friday night jam session—her favorite time of the week.

Singing had always been a passion of hers, one that had been relegated to the back burner as she focused on finishing her veterinary degree. But new city, new rules, new Zara. After arriving in New York, she had answered a classified ad in the *Village Voice* for a band in search of a singer. At the audition, she'd met Ollie, Miguel, and Wally, in a converted warehouse in Long Island City. They'd ended up picking her over half a dozen other candidates.

Out of her three bandmates, it was Ollie who she had warmed to the quickest. He played guitar, wrote songs, and his gentle blue eyes were constantly blinking out SOS signals to the world. After rehearsal, when Wally and Miguel invariably made a beeline for the closest bar, she would always grab dinner with Ollie. Just as friends, of course. He was quite handsome in his rumpled, American guitar boy, kind of way. But she had sworn off men for the near future.

At each stop they gained a few new passengers. Mostly commuters like herself, on their way to Manhattan. But at one of these stops, Zara was surprised to see three mariachis step on, all of them dressed in black from their cowboy hats down to their boots. Two of the men were clutching guitars, and they all started in on a song as the train began to move again. Zara was entranced by their rich voices and deft guitar skills. This was exactly what she loved about New York. One minute the subway car had been this dreary underworld, and the next it was transformed into an impromptu concert.

Finished with their first song, the mariachis struck up a

fresh tune as they walked down in her direction, collecting donations. As they drew closer, Zara saw eyepatch guy fish a five-dollar bill from his pocket, which he slipped into an outstretched hat. The men were all smiles and kicked their playing up a notch. Zara was left wondering if she would ever figure out this perplexing city.

3. AXZLEPROVA

[7:30 a.m.]

The ship remained parked, unnoticed, smack dab in the middle of an open rooftop in one of the most densely packed cities on the planet. During that time the alien went about its business in a conscientious manner. For all the risks, it made sense for them to land in such a crowded area, as opposed to an isolated farm or a barren desert, because there was really no point in traveling light-years just to sit in the middle of nowhere, bored out of your spongy alien mind.

This particular extraterrestrial was named AxzleProva. The head on the right belonged to a male known as Axzle, while the other one belonged to a female named Prova. Neither Axzle nor Prova dwelled very much on whether they were best thought of as one individual with two heads, or two individuals with a shared shell, since in their native tongue anything less than four was considered singular.

AxzleProva had been tasked by the Amalgamation with identifying intelligent life on planet Earth. But the job wasn't as simple as reaching out and tapping the most technologically advanced species on the shoulder. There were specific criteria that had to be met, and the prevailing opinion regarding Earth's dominant species—the warlike and environmentally reckless Homo sapiens—was that they were potentially a class three infestation and that it would be a good idea to keep a close eye on them.

AxzleProva had come to Earth not because of humans, but rather in spite of them. Their mission was to focus on one of the other more promising candidates on the list. The particular species assigned to them was the fur-covered quadruped known to Earth biologists as Felis catus, but referred to locally as a house cat. This clever parasitic species had figured out how to get humans to cater to them night and day. While clearly predators and occasionally aggressive, they were not warlike, and they spent most of their free time dozing peacefully, an attribute that was known to be heavily favored by the Inclusion Committee.

AxzleProva's job involved making detailed evaluations, and if the moment presented itself, they had clearance to initiate contact. This had been attempted once or twice before by other operatives, and the unanimous conclusion, highlighted in the field notes, was that these domestic cats were to be considered highly skittish.

Of the two of them Prova was the more cautious, and she was reluctant to commit to first contact because of the risks involved, whereas Axzle was eager to take advantage of any opportunity to engage. It was not the first time they

had failed to see eye to eye on critical issues. A fed up Prova
had given Axzle the silent treatment for nearly a whole light-
year on the journey over. She had gotten upset with him
for impulsively steering the ship through an asteroid belt for
what he considered a significant shortcut. He had refused
to admit his mistake, maddeningly pointing out that they'd
made it through in one piece. His recklessness had raised
serious questions in Prova's mind about what it meant to go
through life stuck with a foolhardy shell-mate like Axzle.
It wasn't easy to make judicious decisions when you were
literally joined at the hip to someone who behaved like an
overgrown child.

But the successful progress of their mission had put
them both in better moods, and she'd been reminded of how
rewarding it could be to share an adventure like this together.
Of course Axzle still needed to work on his impulse control,
and she would have to keep a close eye on him to make sure
he didn't pull any ill-advised stunts.

At the moment they were partaking of a breakfast made
up of reconstituted marsh shoots—a regrettable staple for
them on missions. While they ate, they were discussing an
unfortunate incident from the night before, which threatened
to prove a serious setback for their research. Axzle was doing
most of the talking, even when his mouth was full, waving
two arms about for increased emphasis. He was in mid-
gesture when a flashing red light and an urgent beeping
alerted them to a breach of the ship's sensor field.

They glanced at the monitor, and their suspicions were
confirmed. This was not the first time the alarm bell had
sounded. Since their arrival it had been triggered several

times a day, waking them from sleep, interrupting their work and their meals.

This repeat offender was visible on the screen—a pigeon, innocently perched on the very highest point of the ship. This was not supposed to happen. They couldn't allow birds or insects to make themselves at home on the ship's exterior. Which was why they were equipped with the most advanced organism repulsors available—cognitive wards, anti-pheromone scents, obnoxious infrared rays and ultrasonic devices. Keeping local vermin away from the vessel shouldn't even be an issue. Yet for some reason this pigeon was still soiling the ship's high tech surface with its sticky excrement. The nose of the ship concealed various important sensors that were critical to entry into planetary atmospheres. Having them covered in pigeon muck was a potentially catastrophic concern.

AxzleProva had already exhausted the various tweaks and intensity adjustments available to their wards, and nothing had worked for this bird. This pigeon had taken a liking to his perch, and was making a mockery of their sophisticated defenses.

Axzle was spitting mad about it. He had never been the most patient turtle in the swamp, and it was all Prova could do to calm him down and remind him of the strict regulations against causing harm to local life-forms. No matter how stubborn and annoying this bird was, they simply couldn't allow things to escalate to the level of physical violence.

In desperation Axzle suggested that they take a little stroll outside and look this bird in the eye so that it would have some notion of its proximity to fierce extraterrestrial beings. He pointed out that it was well-documented that local fauna often found encounters with off-planet species highly alarming.

"You mean we should go outside in broad daylight?" asked Prova. "Are you out of your mind?"

"Listen, shell of my shell, you do realize we are i-n-v-i-s-i-b-l-e?" he replied. Prova did not much care for his tone. She was not the one floating ridiculous ideas. She reminded him that their guidelines clearly stated that they were to limit excursions to nocturnal hours. He pointed out that this was a flexible rule. She said it would never work. And he countered that everything else they'd tried so far had failed.

"Listen, my shell-mate," she said bluntly. "This Earth pigeon has found a spot he likes, and I don't think he would so much as blink if we climbed on the ship and got in his face. He is just not going to budge."

"Well, my darling shell-sharer—there is only one way to find out!"

Compromise was the norm on their home planet. Prova just wished Axzle would meet her halfway sometimes. But after a heated back-and-forth she grew resigned to the fact that Axzle was dead set on trying this approach, whatever the risks, so she relented. They would not be visible, except for their eyeballs, so she had to admit that the chances of being noticed during a brief interaction with the local pest was negligible. She only hoped Axzle was not planning on swatting at the dumb bird.

Axzle strapped the cloaked utility belt to their waist. It contained any number of emergency tools. They slid open the main exit panel just enough to slip outside, their skin quickly adjusting to match their surroundings. Grabbing on to the narrow ladder they began their short climb to the cone-shaped roof. The pigeon made a gurgling noise. Whether or not this meant he was aware of their presence Prova couldn't be sure.

Prova, her eyes the narrowest of slits, stayed alert to all possible threats. Maintaining secrecy and staying unobtrusive was paramount to the success of their mission. Slowly they approached the top, getting closer and closer to the obstinate bird. Prova was particularly concerned about a young male human she spotted standing on a nearby fire escape. And when she turned to alert Axzle, she was shocked to see that he had pulled a blaster from a pocket of their cloaked utility belt.

Instantly she understood his plan. He must have hidden the gun there while he was on watch duty, when she had been fast asleep. He had been planning this for hours, and his intentions were horrifyingly clear. She attempted to gain control of the hand holding the weapon, but Axzle rebuffed her as he was dominant on that side. In desperation she reached over with the free arm she did control and grabbed at his arm, attempting to stop him from raising the weapon. This maneuver infuriated Axzle, and they struggled briefly.

Prova could not believe it had come to this. A physical altercation with her own shell-mate on the surface of an alien planet. The shame was almost too much to bear. To make matters worse, staying camouflaged required utmost concentration, so as they grappled they suddenly became fully visible to the outside world.

It took Prova a few moments to realize that their camouflage had been compromised. With no good options left she immediately gave in to Axzle and did her best to refocus her attention on their concealment. A triumphant Axzle leveled the weapon directly at the pigeon. The bird looked at them curiously, cooed, and cocked his head. The fact that they had materialized out of thin air right next to him did not seem to bother him one bit. Axzle leveled the blaster right at him, and the pigeon cooed once more. Prova wasn't sure what the cognitive capacity of this bird was, but he clearly did not know a gun when he saw one. Axzle pulled the trigger, and the pigeon was instantly vaporized. A few stray feathers floated down to the roof below.

Invisible once more, they made their way back down the side of the tower. Prova was fuming. She had never been so furious in her life. She could not believe Axzle would pull a stunt like this. It was harebrained conduct like this that made local species justifiably paranoid about off world beings. Their whole mission was on the line because of Axzle's vengeful behavior. He had smashed every Amalgamation rule and made a mockery of everything that the Department for Interspecies Contact stood for. How she had ever let herself become attached to a shell-mate like him was a complete mystery to her.

4. OLLIE

[7:45 a.m.]

Before leaving for work, Ollie decided he would take a look out on the fire escape for his missing cat. He pulled on his combat boots, pushed the window up as far as it would go, and slipped outside, scrambling to his feet. It was a cool October morning and the sun, indifferent to the problems of the world, was peeping out above the city rooftops into a patchy sky. Standing there on the rickety fire escape, his view was of the row of buildings north of him on Fifth Street, and of the garden area between them. He often came out here to climb the skinny ladder leading up to the roof, with his guitar strapped to his back and a couple of beers tucked into his pockets. On the roof, he would sit leaning against a wall and experiment with guitar riffs against the backdrop of the humming metropolis.

But Pirate always went down, not up. Ollie tightened his

grip on the blistered iron railing as he leaned over the edge and peered at the ground five stories beneath him, scanning the greenery for any signs of black-and-white fur. Nothing. A rush of vertigo swept over him, but he held himself steady as his eyes darted from overgrown bushes to rusting patio furniture, to long abandoned bikes, searching for any signs of the missing tomcat. Righting himself, the dizziness was replaced by an unexpected wave of outrage. He had trusted that fleabag to enjoy his freedom with the understanding that he would return home safely each night.

"I'm going to strangle that cat when I find him," he said out loud. Mixed in with his anger was a heavy dose of guilt, and the two emotions grappled with each other like crack wrestlers, each gaining the upper hand one moment, and losing it the next.

Everything was quiet at this early hour. It was just him and the wind rustling through the leaves of the old elm tree. Its thick limbs stretched out in all directions, bumping up against fire escapes on both sides. These limbs were Pirate's main conduit to different corners of the garden. Cats were not known for their tree-climbing skills, but no one had bothered to tell Pirate this. For the steeper bits he turned around and shimmied down tailfirst. His friend Zara had taken one look at Pirate and proclaimed him a Norwegian Forest cat—a breed that was notorious for climbing trees. Zara had also told him—repeatedly—that installing a cat flap in his window was a terrible idea. They'd argued about it, and she had used the word negligent. He had retorted that her views were paternalistic. He had simply refused to lock Pirate up in his cramped apartment all day.

Over the past few months Zara had become his closest friend in New York. She was kind, and even though she was incredibly bright, she was never condescending. He wished he could call her right now and tell her Pirate was missing. But she was probably on her way to work. Even if he could reach her, he knew he was bound to get an earful from her about responsible pet ownership.

Church bells echoed through the neighborhood, it was eight o'clock already, and he was going to be late for work himself. Until recently he had only worked afternoons and evenings, but his boss had just reassigned him to the opening shift at the bookstore, a decision Ollie suspected they would both come to regret.

"Oh, Pirate, where have you disappeared to?" he muttered to himself. "Come back already, you stupid cat."

He was about to head back inside when movement on a nearby rooftop caught his eye. There was a figure clinging to a ladder on the side of a water tower on his left, about thirty feet away. He'd always had sharp eyes, but the image that was being transmitted back to his brain was so bizarre that he couldn't make sense of it right away. What the heck was this strange creature? A giant two-headed, four-armed, turtle? Jesus. It was standing on two legs and seemed to be caught up in a weird internal struggle with itself on the tower's ladder. It had to be some sort of costume, right? Maybe they were filming a movie? But there was no crew or cameras in sight, and the two heads were just so incredibly lifelike. They seemed to be furious with each other, and the turtle's two free arms were engaged in wild, combative motions.

Ollie rubbed his eyes. But when he looked back up, the

angry two-headed turtle was still there, grasping the ladder, clear as day. Alarmed, he noticed it was clutching some sort of shiny firearm in one of its many hands, which seemed to be the focus of the struggle. Moments later the dispute was over and the turtle leveled the business end of the weapon at a pigeon who was perched innocently on the tip of the tower. Ollie gasped.

The gun discharged with a zapping sound, and the bird imploded in a puff of feathers. One of the turtle's heads glared at the other. And then the creature simply winked out of sight.

5. AXZLEPROVA

[9 a.m.]

Axzle found himself having to cope with the silent treatment yet again. Prova's last vow of silence had come after he'd steered them through the asteroid belt. And that stretch of quietude had set a new record. He certainly hoped she would thaw more quickly this time around. He was a sociable fellow, and he needed someone to converse with. He considered it cruel of her to cut off communication with him when they were out here all alone, just the two of them. But leave it to Prova to use silence as a weapon. She, on the other hand, didn't seem to mind being stuck in her own head for days on end.

He dearly wished his shell-mate would get over this mania of hers for always doing everything by the book. Who was going to miss one stupid pigeon anyway? The bird was inconsequential, except in as much as it had affected their vessel.

From an ethical standpoint, zapping him was no different from inadvertently stepping on one of those cockroaches that liked to crisscross the rooftop at night.

True, they had been conspicuously visible to that human male for a brief moment. That was regrettable. But it was Prova's fault, really. If she had not turned and attacked him, then it would not have happened. But he had no hope of ever getting her to see it that way. Prova did not seem to understand that a critical element of remote planet fieldwork involved off-the-script improvisation. Protocol on its own could not be expected to cope with every possible eventuality.

"Honestly, the fuss you're making over that feathered pest, I just do not get it." Axzle punched a few buttons on the panel in front of them. "And I would not worry too much about that human male. As you know, it is extremely common for observers to assume that what they are seeing is not real."

Prova typed furiously on the keypad in the arm of her chair. With a sigh, Axzle read her words off the screen in front of him:

Well, what if he does not? What if he goes to the authorities and we are faced with an armed military response?

"Unlikely," Axzle countered with a smug smile. "But if it turns out we have to leave the planet in a hurry, we will stage a quick exit. Human technology is still very primitive compared to ours."

Prova glared at him and stabbed at her keyboard angrily:

You are an abominable shell-mate.

Axzle shrugged.

6. OLLIE

[11:15 a.m.]

The sense of gloom that he'd felt in his apartment seemed to have attached itself to him on his walk to work, following him around like one of those mini rain clouds you see in cartoons. Ollie considered himself an upbeat guy, but at the moment he couldn't shake the feeling that he had been singled out as the butt of some weird cosmic joke.

He was still trying to digest the scene he had witnessed earlier on the fire escape. Years ago he had watched a documentary about ancient Egypt that had pushed the idea that extraterrestrials had been behind the construction of the pyramids, and ever since Ollie had placed himself firmly in the pro-alien visitation camp. But that was quite different from actually seeing an alien creature vaporize a pigeon on a New York rooftop with your own two eyes. This firsthand experience made extraterrestrials seem all too real. Added to this was a nagging worry that this ray gun-toting space turtle might be connected to Pirate's disappearance. It was a deeply unsettling thought.

His friends frequently accused him of having an overactive imagination. And for a second he'd wondered if he had somehow hallucinated the whole thing. But it wasn't as if he was on some sort of peyote-induced vision quest. He had been standing on a fire escape first thing in the morning, with a perfectly clear head. There was nothing hazy or nebulous about what he'd observed. He had seen a giant two-headed turtle holding a ray gun, which it had fired at a poor pigeon, obliterating it. Then the giant turtle had simply vanished into thin air. So far he had not been able to come up with any credible alternative explanations to his alien landing theory.

Lost in thought, he soon arrived at the Book Cave. Located on the corner of Lafayette and Tenth Street, it was a multistory downtown mecca for booklovers that provided him with a regular paycheck. The place had a timeworn industrial feel, with iron columns spaced throughout the store, tube lights dangling overhead, and ceilings that were crisscrossed by heating ducts and ventilation shafts, bolted in place in defiance of gravity. It was always quietly busy, the soft hum of activity mixing with the sound of faintly piped classical music.

Ollie clocked in late and got himself yelled at by the store manager, Mr. Bartok, who announced he was "on thin ice" and banished him upstairs to the music section, an area on the third floor dedicated to used records, tapes, and CDs. Mr. Bartok was a squat, bald man with a dark bushy beard and odd tufts of hair protruding from his ears and nostrils. Ollie knew Mr. Bartok would be shadowing him today, and that any little mistake could land him in hot water.

Minutes later, Ollie stood behind the counter in the music section, slipping record albums into plastic sleeves and slapping them with a price tag. He was having a hard time concentrating because his mind kept flashing back to the rooftop visitant. He needed to talk to someone about this. Ollie realized that keeping it to himself would drive him crazy. But how was he supposed to broach the subject of an alien sighting in conversation? People would think he'd flipped his lid.

Out of all his fellow bookstore minions, his two best friends were Miguel and Wally, who both happened to be working today. And they weren't just his work buddies, either, they were also his bandmates. Miguel was a wildman on the drums, and Wally was a reliable presence on the bass guitar. Zara was their main vocalist of course, lending the band a touch of British cred and some feminine style. For his part Ollie played guitar, sang backup, and threw some occasional keyboard stylings into the mix.

Around midmorning Miguel and Wally stopped by the music counter for a chat. He could tell they had taken note of the rather peculiar expression on his face because they asked him right away if he had something on his mind. But even though Ollie was dying to unburden himself, he wasn't sure these two friends were the right audience for his news. He suspected he would just be setting himself up for ridicule. The jokes would start and then just keep coming, quite possibly for years.

He did his best to just play it cool. But his friends weren't buying it.

"You've had a funny look about you all day," insisted Miguel, who was a skinny little guy with a skimpy mustache and a bushy tuft of hair knotted on top of his head.

"Yeah, Ollie, something is definitely going on with you today, man," proclaimed Wally, who was built like a line-backer, but had a gentle disposition.

"Well, my cat has gone missing," said Ollie. "So I'm a bit upset about that."

Wally shook his head sadly. "That's too bad, man."

"He's an outdoor cat, right?" asked Miguel. "What do you think happened to him?"

"I'm not sure, but he has missed a couple of meals at this point, and I'm getting pretty worried."

"Hey, man, keep the faith," said Wally. "He probably caught himself a squirrel or somethin' and he's binged out under a bush somewhere."

"I'm not sure that's it. I was out on my fire escape this morning and there was no sign of him anywhere." Ollie considered for a moment, and then decided to take the plunge. He needed to tell someone, badly. "I did see something pretty strange when I was standing there though." Ollie spoke in a hushed tone and his two friends leaned in. "You guys are not going to believe it."

"What is it? Spit it out already, man," said Wally.

In spite of his misgivings, Ollie told them all about the strange creature on the water tower ladder, the vaporized pigeon, and the way the space turtle had simply vanished. His two friends exchanged incredulous looks.

"I guess you was right," said Miguel. "We don't believe it."

"Not one word. A space tortoise?" said Wally.

"Tortoise, turtle, I don't know what it was. It was green and it had a shell."

"And two heads, you say?" asked Miguel.

"Yep, both coming out of the one shell. And I don't know what to tell you—it's the honest-to-god truth."

"Don't you think that if aliens had landed in the East Village this morning that we would've heard about it on the news?" Miguel pointed out.

"Yeah," said Wally. "It seems like the kind of thing that would make the headlines."

Ollie shrugged. "Maybe I'm the only one who saw it?"

"Wait a second," said Miguel. "Let me get this straight. Do you think this space turtle has something to do with your missing cat?"

"I'm worried that it does. That poor pigeon was toast. You ever seen a living thing get vaporized? It sticks in your mind, I can tell you that."

Miguel stared at him quizzically. "Err . . . You wasn't like popping shrooms for breakfast or something?"

"Or maybe you hit your head?" asked Wally.

"No, and no. I feel fine. Look, I saw what I saw. Okay? And it was real. I swear it." His friends regarded him silently.

Just then, Miguel's expression changed. He'd caught sight of someone out of the corner of his eye. "Bartok, closing in at nine o'clock," he hissed.

"Keep all of this between us," Ollie whispered as his friends made themselves scarce.

Mr. Bartok informed Ollie that he needed him to go stock shelves in the History section with incoming titles. He gave Mr. Bartok a "sure thing boss," and trudged down to the second floor. He filled a handcart in the stockroom, wheeled it over to the towering bookcases, and spent the next hour going up and down a ladder shelving books in hard to reach places.

There wasn't much room to squeeze past his ladder in the narrow aisle, so any customers who strayed his way in the maze of bookshelves would stop and circle around. Until, that is, a teenage girl in a purple hoodie appeared, who seemed completely undeterred by the ladder blocking her path. With a dazed look in her eyes, and headphones blaring from somewhere under her curly hair, she plowed onward. He couldn't believe it—did she even see him up here? He set down the book he was holding—A Comprehensive Guide to the Peloponnesian War—on the top cap of the ladder, nervously grabbing onto a metal brace that connected the neighboring bookcases to one another at their highest points. As the girl brushed by, the book shifted slightly, teetered on the edge for a moment, and then tipped over. Ollie made a mad grab for it but was too late, and he watched helplessly as it hurtled toward the figure below. Thankfully, after a brief struggle, the girl had squeezed past, and, taking a short step down the aisle, moved out of the path of the falling hardcover in the nick of time. The weighty tome landed with a thud, right where she'd been stuck a split second earlier.

Ollie was mortified—that was close. A few customers nearby had glanced over at the sound of the book hitting the floor, but they quickly resumed their browsing. Even the girl who had very nearly become the latest casualty of the Peloponnesian War went on her way without so much as a backward glance.

Ollie scurried down the ladder and scooped up the stray tome. But when he straightened up, he found himself face-to-face with Mr. Bartok. Wispy eyebrows raised and half-moon glasses lowered, his boss fixed him with a penetrating stare and said the words Ollie had been dreading:

"Oliver, I'd like to see you in my office, please. Now."

Ollie shuffled dejectedly after the stocky man, letting himself be led downstairs, toward the back of the store, and finally down the narrow hallway that led to a small office. His coworkers shot him sympathetic glances along the way.

"Shut the door, please," Mr. Bartok said, his face locked in a frown.

"Oliver. I'd prefer it if you refrained from injuring the customers by dropping books on their heads. They are less likely to sue the store and bankrupt us all if we allow them to leave the premises without the need for a stretcher."

"Yes, sir. I'm really sorry. It slipped off the top of the ladder. It won't happen again."

"You're damn right it wont!" Mr. Bartok had worked himself up to shouting mode, and he emphasized this last remark by pounding a fist on his desk. "You come in atrociously late and wander around the store in a daze. Do you think I pay you to stare into space? Because I don't!" The manager's desk took the brunt of another serious blow. "Do you have anything to say for yourself?" If there was one thing Ollie was sure of, it was that Mr. Bartok didn't want to hear a story about a missing cat or a giant space turtle.

"Clean out your locker. You're fired. Effective immediately. You can expect your last paycheck in the mail."

Minutes later Miguel and Wally cornered him in the

back room, and they must have been eavesdropping because they already seemed to know he'd been canned.

"Hey, Ollie," said Miguel, who seemed almost teary-eyed. "We heard about what happened. This really sucks. We're real sorry to see you go."

"Yep, we gonna miss you around here, that's for sure," added Wally, shaking his head morosely. "I can't believe it."

"At least I have the afternoon off to go look for Pirate," Ollie said, trying to put a brave face on, even though he was feeling panicked. Without a job, he was worried New York would just kick him to the curb like yesterday's garbage. But before he could tackle that problem, he had to find Pirate. "I'm gonna go grab an early lunch. Call Zara for me, will ya? Tell her I probably won't be there tonight. Just say I'm taking care of something. Please don't tell her about Pirate, or about getting fired, and definitely don't mention that other thing I told you about earlier. Okay?"

Miguel nodded reassuringly and patted him on the shoulder.

7. ZARA

[11:15 a.m.]

As a young girl, Zara had brought home every injured creature and abandoned pet she'd stumbled across. Her mother had despaired, faced with a menagerie that at one point had included a cat, a rabbit, a chinchilla, a parakeet, a Siamese fighting fish, and a gecko. But Zara never neglected any of her charges, rushing home every day after school and nursing them back to health. Her childhood dream had been to be a zookeeper when she grew up.

And here she was now, in the midst of her third clinical rotation at the Lower East Side Animal Hospital in New York, the final requirement for her Veterinary Science degree. She could hardly believe the finish line was in sight. She was currently assigned to emergency care, which sometimes meant dealing with dire cases, but so far today it had just been a steady trickle of anxious pet owners rushing in with vomiting dogs who had chowed down on chocolate, or queasy cats who had been nibbling on toxic plants. None of them beyond repair.

By far her most memorable examination this morning had involved a large boa with three strange lumps in its midsection. An X-ray had quickly solved the mystery. Zara had informed the startled owner, whose husband was an avid indoor golf aficionado, that the snake had swallowed three golf balls, no doubt confusing them for eggs. She'd assured her that they wouldn't do the snake any harm.

Zara was taking care of paperwork in the back room while chatting with her fellow intern Jeannie, a spunky girl with short-cropped black hair and a sprinkle of freckles around her nose. Jeannie was going clubbing with her girlfriends later tonight and she invited Zara along. Zara explained that she had a band jam session.

"You know, Zara, I really don't get this karaoke and beer thing you are into on the weekends."

"Excuse me?" said Zara indignantly. "We play real music!"

"If you say so. Hey, isn't that guy Ollie in the band? The one you like to go out to dinner with? Just the two of you?"

"Yeah, he's our ringleader."

"So is he like your boyfriend then? I thought you were single?" Jeannie was prone to rapid-fire questions.

"Ollie and I are just friends. I don't have time for dating right now," Zara said with a tight smile.

"Is he one of those pipe-dream types?"

Zara bristled. "The world needs musicians, Jeannie. Just like it needs vets, and firemen, and plumbers."

"Are you sure you aren't just a little bit sweet on this Ollie? Kind of sounds like you are to me."

"No. He's just easy to talk to. He gets me. I wouldn't want things to get complicated."

"Maybe he's madly in love with you and you don't know it?"

"I'm pretty sure he isn't," said Zara in a clipped tone.

"Well, have fun tonight with your *boyfriend*!" Jeannie grinned. "And if you ever want to join me and the girls on a Friday, I can guarantee you an evening of drunkenness and debauchery."

"Wow, drunkenness *and* debauchery," Zara parroted. She didn't appreciate Jeannie's insinuations that there might be something more going on between her and Ollie. Clearly she didn't understand about guy friends. Zara was determined to stick to her plan and take a nice long break from boys while she was in New York. Romantically speaking, that is. But as friends went, her three bandmates had turned out to be an interesting bunch. And there was none of the drama, gossip, or backstabbing that were all but inevitable with girlfriends.

As painful as her breakup with Richard had been, it was really her best friend Darby who had let her down the most. Darby, who had neglected to tell her about Richard's revolving door of party girls. Darby, who had encouraged her to look the other way because Richard was the kind of man who had the world at his feet. Zara couldn't believe it. Was expecting her boyfriend to be a decent human being really so much to ask? She didn't feel as though she had set the bar that high.

Zara wondered what Darby would think of Ollie.

Richard and Ollie were about as night and day as you could possibly get. Darby would likely sniff disdainfully at scruffy Ollie, with his rockstar dreams, and bookstore day job. Even Zara's own parents would probably think Ollie wasn't good enough for their little girl. Mum and Dad were sweethearts, but snobbish sweethearts. She tried to imagine the look on her parents' faces if she were ever to introduce him. They would take one look at Ollie and make the same sour expressions they'd made when her ten-year-old self brought an injured toad home with her from a camping trip.

She wasn't sure what Ollie would think about her London life either. She had been vague about the details with him. She didn't want him to think she was some sort of spoiled Euro-princess. She'd told him that her dad was a doctor, and her mom was a lawyer, but she'd skipped the part about them both being at the top of their fields and owning a three-story townhouse just off Hyde Park. With an indoor pool in the basement. And she'd avoided mentioning her breakup with a playboy upper-cruster entirely.

Finished with her paperwork, Zara was making the rounds to check on some of her patients in the holding area when she heard her name being called over the intercom by reception. This was worrisome. She made a beeline for the front desk, where Katrina, the skinny Russian receptionist, waved her over.

"Hey, Zara, I have a friend of yours on the line. Says his name is Miguel? I can patch him through to the phone by the water cooler, if you like."

"Thanks, I'll go pick up right now."

"Isn't she just the cutest?" Katrina directed this last

comment about Zara to her fellow receptionist, who hummed her agreement. Zara rolled her eyes as she hurried off down the hall. She got this a lot. The main culprit—the reason people often treated her like an overachieving grade schooler—was her button nose, which steered her like a laser guided missile into the cute box every time. Her shoulder-length brown hair, her big brown eyes, and her petite figure did nothing to counteract this schoolgirl impression. She'd inherited her caterpillar eyebrows from her dad, and they were her one serious note, helping her pull off a piercing stare when needed.

Zara picked up the receiver and punched the button with the red light over it.

"Zara speaking."

Miguel quickly filled her in on the news that Pirate was missing. She wasn't the least bit surprised really. She had given Ollie a hard time when she'd found out about the pet door in his fire escape window. She knew he liked to think of the garden space behind his flat as a magical backyard for Pirate to play in, far removed from the dangers of the city streets, but that was just foolishness.

But Miguel wasn't done yet. He said there was more, and that he and Wally were worried about Ollie.

"Why? What else is the matter?"

"Well, for one thing, he got the ax at the bookstore."

"You mean he got fired?"

"Yep."

"How did that happen?"

"Bad luck, I think. The boss is in a foul mood today. Somebody was bound to get it in the neck."

"Wow. Poor Ollie. That's awful."

"Sure is. But there's more."

"Seriously?"

"Yeah, and this last one is the real zinger." Zara couldn't imagine what could be worse than losing a pet and getting let go at work. Then Miguel told her about Ollie's sighting on the fire escape.

"Wait, what?" she stammered, startled by what she thought she'd heard.

"Ollie said he saw an extraterrestrial up on the roof this morning."

"Surely he was just pulling your leg?"

"This was no prank. He was dead serious. He's convinced he saw an alien zap a pigeon on a rooftop this morning. And me and Wally are pretty sure he's gone off his rocker."

Zara had no idea what to say. She didn't want to jump to conclusions without talking to Ollie first. In the end she promised Miguel she would track Ollie down at his usual lunch place, and that she would do her best to get to the bottom of things.

8. OLLIE

[12:00 p.m.]

He was sitting alone at a small table by the window. Nico's was a tiny sliver of a place, with a checkered floor, and a casual vibe. It didn't have the best pizza in town, but Ollie came here because he could get two slices and a soda for three bucks. Gazing absently through the glass window, Ollie was startled to spot Zara crossing the street, headed his way. What was she doing here? Her hair was pulled back into a loose tie, and she had her hands balled up in the sleeves of an oversized yellow sweater that she had pulled on over her scrubs. She looked pretty as ever, but Ollie knew that hiding behind that sweet exterior lurked a fiery personality. He sensed that Miguel might've spilled the beans about Pirate being missing, and if he had, then Zara would be in a real huff. She could get extremely worked up about animal safety.

She looked at him questioningly when she came through

the door. Ollie swallowed hard and croaked out a nervous greeting.

"Miguel said I would find you here," she stated matter-of-factly.

Ollie had a few moments to steel himself while she went up to the counter to order herself a slice. Then she plopped down in the chair opposite him.

"So. I hear Pirate is missing."

Ollie was going to have some choice words to share with Miguel next time he saw him. "Yeah, he's disappeared. I haven't seen him since last night."

Warily, he filled her in on the details of Pirate's disappearance, but she didn't blow up at him, or accuse him of being a lousy pet owner, or bludgeon him with the napkin holder. She just sat there calmly, staring back at him with worried eyes. Which was weird. He had braced himself for riled-up Zara, not for this quietly sympathetic impostor. Was she waiting for him to drop his guard?

Zara broke the silence by telling him the story of how she lost her dog when she was eleven, but found him safe and sound two days later.

"So, the whole lost pet thing," she said, "I've been there."

Another dose of commiseration. Ollie frowned. Clearly this was how she intended to play her cards. He chewed on his lip as he pondered his response. "Well at least you weren't to blame for your dog escaping," he said pointedly. If she wasn't going to engage, then he would just have to draw the real Zara out into the open.

"Well, neither are you." Zara mumbled unconvincingly. "It's just . . . unfortunate."

"Nothing more than bad luck, you mean?" Ollie locked eyes with her.

"Well you have to admit it was pretty foolish to let Pirate outside in the first place, right?" she said, a hint of exasperation in her voice.

"Of course I know that. And I feel terrible about it, okay? What do you want me to say? You were right all along! Is that what you want to hear?" He sat there sullenly.

"What I want, *Ollie*, is for you to listen to me before-hand. That's all."

"Well it's too late for beforehands now, isn't it?"

"But it's not too late for you to stop being such a twit," she said, glowering at him. He was about to reply petulantly that he could be a twit, whatever that was, if he wanted to be one, but just then the guy behind the counter called out that her slice was ready. Ollie pushed back his chair and got up to fetch it for her.

Zara took a bite, fearless in the face of dripping cheese. Then she made a face. "Honestly, Ollie," Zara whispered, "of all the pizza places in the city, I don't know why you have to come here. We have better pizza in London, and our pizza is terrible."

"It helps to go heavy on the free condiments." He nudged the garlic powder and red pepper jars in her direction.

Zara scrunched her nose up at this suggestion. "I gotta head back to work in a few," she said, "so let's get back to Pirate. I take it he's not wearing a collar, and he's never been chipped?"

"Bingo."

"Well, there are still some things we can do. Have you thought about making flyers?"

"Flyers?"

"Yeah, you know, missing cat posters?"

"Ah yes. I did think that might be a good idea at some point."

"Well, guess what—that time is now."

"I have the afternoon off—long story, don't ask—so I'll get right on it."

"Actually, I've already heard about you being let go by the bookstore," she said softly.

Now Ollie was even more annoyed at his bandmates. "Who knew Miguel was such a blabbermouth!"

"How did it happen?" she asked. "Miguel didn't have time to go into the details."

Ollie explained about getting to work late, and nearly braining a teenage girl with a weighty history volume.

"Well, don't worry. There are plenty of other jobs in this city."

"Yeah, I'm more concerned about Pirate at the moment."

"I'll stop by your place when I get off work and help you with the search. Around sevenish? And I'll pop into the local shelter on my way over, and see if he's turned up there."

Ollie sat up straight. "Wait, do you think there's any chance of that?"

"Sure. If someone called animal control on him, that's where he would end up."

"I didn't even think of that."

"Well, what was your theory?" Zara asked with a mischievous smile. "Did you think Pirate was abducted by aliens?"

Ollie, who was draining the dregs of his lemonade, nearly choked on his drink. "Why would I think that?" he said in a higher-pitched voice than usual. Was it possible she knew about this too? Had Miguel and Wally really sold him out three times over and then given her a shove in his direction?

"Miguel says you told him and Wally a wild story about having some kind of extraterrestrial sighting this morning?" As she met his eyes, Zara gave her eyebrows a slight questioning lift.

Ollie, who had been reluctant to talk about this with Miguel and Wally, really didn't want to get into it with her. He didn't really care what those two blockheads thought of him, but he cared a lot about what she thought. Still he was in a proper jam now. He couldn't just lie about it. "It's possible I might have said something like that to them," he said finally. "But if I did I'm pretty sure I would have sworn them both to secrecy. And I'd prefer not to talk about it right now."

"Excuse me? You think you saw an alien earlier today, but you don't want to talk about it? I'm sorry, but this is now the subject of conversation, and I'm not going to let you off the hook until you give me some details."

"You're just going to look at me like I've gone crazy."

"Have you gone crazy?"

"No."

"Because you're having quite a dreadful day."

"Don't I know it."

"I promise to listen with an open mind."

Ollie looked around to make sure no one was within eavesdropping distance. There were people coming in and out, but no one was paying them any attention. So he told her about standing on his fire escape, about looking up at the water tower, and about seeing a two-headed creature clinging to the ladder. He told her about the ray gun, the pigeon, and the vanishing into thin air. She listened intently without interrupting.

"Wow. Now on a scale of one to ten how sure are you about what you saw? Was it at all . . . fuzzy?"

"It was just like seeing you here eating pizza. I wish I could say I was drunk, or on drugs, or delirious in some way. But it was all clear as day. Up to the point when the space turtle vanished into thin air, that is. I know how it sounds, believe me. I wouldn't believe a word of it myself if someone else told me. You must think I'm ready to be carted off to the nuthouse."

"No. I don't think that. But I won't say I'm not just a little concerned about your mental health."

"Because you don't believe aliens exist?"

"No, it's not that. It's the part about them popping up on an East Village rooftop this morning that I am struggling with."

"So you would have no trouble believing this creature existed, but you would nitpick about the geography?"

"Now you're twisting my words."

"Well at least I'm not questioning your sanity."

"I'm a bit surprised you're not questioning your own sanity, to be honest. If something like that happened to me, I think I'd make a beeline for the nearest psychiatrist's office."

"I don't trust shrinks. And I don't think I'm crazy. Have you ever stopped to think about how far human civilization has advanced in such a short time. It makes sense to think we've had some outside help."

"Are you insinuating that aliens slipped us the blueprints for TV remotes and microwave ovens?"

"That's just as likely as thinking we came up with that stuff on our own."

"So do you also see some sort of connection between Pirate's disappearance and this giant space turtle?"

"That's what I've been trying to figure out. I mean, if this creature is going around zapping animals left and right, then it's possible it may have taken out Pirate too."

"Well I think it would be wise to proceed under the assumption that Pirate's absence has a more ordinary explanation. And if that doesn't pan out, we can always look into more unorthodox possibilities later."

"Well making flyers covers both bases if you ask me. It's possible some neighbor looking out of a window may have seen this space turtle zap Pirate. Something strange has happened to that cat. I'm sure of it. Pirate wouldn't have just wandered off, or gotten lost."

"At the hospital, we see plenty of cats who have fallen off balconies or been run over by cars. And their owners never saw it coming."

"Pirate is a good climber," Ollie protested. "You said it yourself. And there are no cars in the back courtyard where he hangs out."

She rolled her eyes at him. "Yes, but he can easily get from the gardens to the street," she said loudly. "And the outdoor world has many other dangers for pets."

To Ollie, she sounded like a broken record. "Pirate knows what he's doing," he said firmly.

"Honestly Ollie, you're impossible to reason with. I don't know why I even bother trying to help."

Now she was properly annoyed. Ollie was feeling peeved himself. She clearly didn't believe a word of his story. And just like Miguel and Wally, she was treating him like a dummy. "For the record, I don't remember asking for your help," he snapped.

Zara let loose a guttural *argh!* sound. Her eyes blazed with a mixture of hurt and fury. "You know, you're right. You didn't call me to ask for my help with any of this. And you obviously don't value my advice. I don't know why I even bother!" She stood up abruptly. "I need to get back to work. Good luck finding your damn cat."

Ollie was taken aback. And by the time he'd thought to apologize she was already out the door.

9. MANOLO

[12:00 p.m.]

Manolo Ortiz Molina put the lie to the reputation native New Yorkers had for being loud and brash. He was nothing of the sort—a quiet and humble man, he believed in hard work and good manners. Sadly, these qualities, along with his navy blue coveralls, made it easy for people to look past him, in spite of his bulky build. The main impression he gave people, when they did notice him, was of being square—square shoulders, square head, square jaw. Only his cheeks were round and chubby. A dark shadow of a beard covered large areas of his face, and he liked to tuck his curly hair under a flat cap, both of which helped to obscure him even further from the world.

Manolo had started out as a handyman at a section 8 up in the Bronx, but he'd worked his way up over the years and was now in charge of a mostly rat-free Manhattan building in the Lower East Side. Being a superintendent wasn't everyone's idea of a comfortable life. But most people had not grown up in the South Bronx in the seventies, like he had.

Manolo credited the heroic efforts of his aunt Rita for keeping both him and his sister out of harm's way. She had raised them, and she'd frequently told Manolo and his sister that they were "good as a piece of bread," adding that if they kept their heads down, trouble wouldn't find them. Manolo still felt her presence in his life every day—her kind blue eyes looking down on him, filled to the brim with love. The woman had been a legit saint, as well as the greatest cook in the world, God rest her soul.

The building Manolo was now responsible for was nine stories tall and took up the length of the block on Avenue A between Fourth and Fifth Streets. Running a building this size was an impossibly big job, and a messy one. But Manolo wasn't afraid to get his hands dirty. You had to be able to cope with the non-stop flow of rotting garbage and the stench that came with it. And you had to be quick to grab a plunger and wade into a bathroom overflowing with fresh crap. That was part of the job, a job that paid him a modest salary and allowed him to live rent-free in a decent part of town. And while no one enjoyed the filth, there was a certain pride that came from knowing you were the only one with the stomach to face up to that muck day in and day out. Manolo had no respect for the young college kids who moved into his building without even knowing how to install their top lock. Or the office workers who were making big bucks in mid-town somewhere, but expected him to come running every time they caught a mouse in a goddamn sticky trap. As if it was somehow easier for him to drown the poor creature in a bucket.

His duties as a super sometimes took him to the roof where he would inspect for leaks and check that the boiler chimney was not blocked and that cables and other wires were all properly tied down. Occasionally there would be a dead pigeon to clean up. But most important, he would go up to the roof regularly to inspect the building's water tower, making sure the pump was working correctly and the water level was where it should be. Currently this inspection was weeks overdue, a fact that was weighing heavily on his mind. Yet he couldn't quite bring himself to climb that last flight of stairs to the roof. And he didn't exactly know why.

It wasn't that he was afraid. He'd been on the roof hundreds of times and there was nothing to be afraid of up there. It wasn't that he didn't want to go either, because he hadn't clawed his way up in the building maintenance world by being negligent in his duties. No, it was something else, something he couldn't quite put his finger on. Some unknown reason lodged somewhere in his thick skull that was interfering with his work.

Trying to figure out what was behind this mental block was giving him a big headache. If he had been in a different income bracket, he would have gone to see a shrink. As it was, he couldn't even bring it up to his wife, Natalya, since she would just add it to her long list of his mental deficiencies.

Manolo had taken the elevator to the ninth floor for the second time that day and was standing in front of the stairs leading to the roof, jingling the keys looped on his belt nervously. This had become something of a ritual for him in the past few weeks. He willed himself to stick out a foot and put it on the first step going up. But the message just didn't seem to trickle down to his feet, which remained firmly rooted to the marble floor.

As best he could figure, there was something in his mind—some vague memory or thought—that was preventing him from proceeding upward. Standing there, one flight down, he sensed some strange presence on the roof above him. Some otherworldly force compelling him to stay away. Manolo had never believed in the supernatural, preferring to keep himself grounded in practical matters like mopping floors and fixing radiators.

But, while he hated to admit it, the only explanation he could come up with was that he was dealing with some sort of curse. This was how his aunt had always labeled bad things that couldn't be explained. She would have been convinced that a curse was warning him to keep away, or else bad things would happen.

With a sigh, Manolo turned away and took the stairs, heading down, scanning the steps for any trash as he went. He just didn't get it. He knew he had never been the smartest guy on the block, but by sticking stubbornly to the straight and narrow, he had managed to get ahead in life. But his go-to methods—honesty, hard work, and patience—were failing him. Finding his mental toolbox empty, he was left feeling strangely fearful. Normally, he was never afraid of anything—with the notable exception of Natalya, of course.

Thinking of Natalya did nothing to cheer him up. She was his biggest mistake. He'd been irresistibly drawn to her from the start. A true force of nature, she radiated a powerful

sense of self, much like Aunt Rita had. Natalya had lured him
in with the usual charms—her long blond hair, her curva-
ceous figure, and a seductive smile. But he'd realized too late
that, unlike his aunt, who had been nothing but kind and
good, Natalya had a mean streak a mile wide. She made that
crystal clear soon after their city hall ceremony, but by then
the door had slammed shut behind him. Now he was tied to
a woman who was prone to venomous rants. He felt like one
of those mice caught in a sticky trap—putting out just a tiny
little paw had doomed him forever. And he couldn't help but
wonder if, like those mice, he was now forced to wait for a
slow and drawn-out death. *Or maybe if I'm lucky, God will
send some poor sucker along to drown me mercifully in a bucket?*
The thought made him chuckle quietly to himself.

As Manolo wound his way down the stairs, he wondered
if it would make sense to ask one of the parish priests for
advice about his roof problem. Religion had never gripped
Manolo strongly, but he still went to mass every Sunday out
of habit, and out of respect for his dead aunt. But somehow
he doubted the local pastor would be much help with inexplicable roof curses.

His next thought was that maybe he would ask his sister, Maricela, for help. She was the brains in the family. Of
course, she was also fond of psychics, crystals, and other new
age nonsense. For the past few years, she'd even been caught
up in the worship of Santa Muerte. Manolo considered it very
fortunate Aunt Rita hadn't lived long enough to see that, as
it would've broken her heart. Manolo himself had always
considered Santa Muerte to be a dangerous cult, filled with
criminals and gangsters. But as he slowly wound his way

down to the ground floor, he began to rethink his take on such things. He was feeling strangely open to new possibilities. It occurred to him that his current problem was a better fit for his sister's unorthodox spiritual beliefs. And while he wasn't enthusiastic about the idea, he was desperate. He needed help from somewhere. *Yes,* he thought to himself—*if that's the approach Maricela suggests, I will go along with it. So long as it is handled discreetly, so that I can still take my usual spot in the back of the church on Sundays, with none the wiser.* And of course, not a word of it could reach Natalya, as it would be sure to make her furious. Most things did these days.

10. OLLIE

[1 p.m.]

Twelve months ago, when Ollie stepped off the bus at Port Authority—a wide-eyed twenty-four-year-old from the Midwest with a guitar case and a dream—he had been terrified of the city. He saw dangers lurking around every corner. Over the past year, he'd gradually gotten used to the chaos of city life. But today the streets had reclaimed that initial menacing edge: Workers dismantling scaffolding had turned the sidewalk into a deadly obstacle course. Kamikaze pigeons seemed intent on dive-bombing him. And a taxi cab, ignoring the light, had barreled right past him in the Third Avenue crosswalk, horn blaring.

By the time Ollie got to his building, he was a bundle of nerves. He trudged up the stairs, with little hope of finding Pirate waiting for him at home. When he reached the hall-way on the sixth floor, he noticed his neighbor's door was wide open. His friend Herbert in 6E was an old-timer who had lived in the building for thirty-odd years. Ollie sometimes did small favors for him, like carrying his groceries upstairs. Hearing Ollie's footsteps, Herbert poked his head out of his doorway.

"Hiya, kid! Just who I was hoping to see!" Herbert was a tubby old man, with a fringe of short-cropped white hair, a rounded bristly beard, and a fondness for Hawaiian shirts.

"Hey, Herbert, how are you?" Ollie replied, eyeing his own front door ten feet further down.

"Help me out, will ya, kid? I've been sitting in the dark all day, and the food in my fridge is gonna go bad." Ollie glanced into Herbert's shadowy apartment—if it was just a question of a blown fuse, it should not take long.

"Sure," he said, "but I gotta make it quick today, Herbert."

"What's your rush?" The old man peered up at him. "Hey, you look a little green around the gills. What's eating you?"

"It's a long story."

"You can tell me all about it while you look at my fuse box, then. The last time I climbed on a chair, I nearly broke my hip." Ollie resisted the urge to ask him if he had called the super.

Stepping into Herbert's place always felt like stepping back in time. There was an orange couch and matching drapes, a boomerang-shaped coffee table, and a large wooden box TV with rabbit ears. Ollie tested a couple of light switches in the darkened apartment and pulled the chain on the ceiling fan—nothing. At times like this, Ollie felt bad for the old guy, who didn't have any relatives in the city.

Ollie grabbed a sturdy chair from the kitchen and climbed

up to reach the fuse box, which was high up on a wall filled with framed photographs.

"It's my own fault," Herbert said. "I was running too many appliances at the same time." Ollie nodded. Herbert handed him a small flashlight that cast a feeble beam of light on the switches. Right away he noticed a couple flipped circuit breakers, so he clicked them firmly back into place, and the lights came on instantly in various corners of the small apartment.

Herbert refused to let him leave until he told him why he was looking so dejected. So they sat down at the kitchen table, and Ollie told him about Pirate using the space in the back of the building as his own little stomping grounds, and not returning home last night.

"That's a tough break, kid. I'm real sorry to hear it. I can tell your cat means a lot to you. It's easy to get lost in this crazy city. Heck, it's easy to get lost anywhere. Did I ever tell you about the time I was visiting my cousin Henri down in the Bayou and we lost a tourist in the swamp—"

"Maybe save this one for another day Herbert, because—" But the old man was already forging ahead.

"My cousin and I were having breakfast when he got a call from a neighbor asking us to join a search party for an out-of-towner who'd gone missing. Apparently this stranger had shown up in town the day before and ducked into the local watering hole, where he was drawn into a poker game with some regulars. People in those parts loved to bamboozle visitors, and this guy seemed like easy pickings. They distracted him from their underhanded tricks by telling him a whopper about a huge albino gator that lived in a distant corner of the swamp, a fifteen-footer who the locals had dubbed the

Ghost Croc. Now it turns out this guy was a photographer for a magazine, and he got it into his head to try and track down this creature. Come morning they rented him a battered wooden canoe, charged him extra for the paddle of course, and threw in a life vest and a container of gumbo for free, to even out the score a little. And off he went into the swamp alone, with a map in his pocket sketched out on a bar napkin, and a camera hanging from his neck like an anvil.

"Everyone knew this was a bad idea. It was too easy to get all turned around in the swamp. But no one said anything because people back then knew how to mind their own business. Still, no one was terribly surprised when he didn't return by nightfall, and when there was still no sign of him the next day, people began to fret. Some were worried about his safety, others more concerned with recovering the rented canoe, and some pointed out that if anyone came looking for him, they might ask uncomfortable questions about their hospitality.

"So they called us, and anyone else who was free, to help comb the swamp. We set out in three separate fan boats in search of this guy, or what was left of him. The first thing we found was his life vest. Not a good sign. But some of us figured he may have taken it off on account of the heat and lost it overboard. The next thing we found was the paddle. Even the most hopeful among us had to admit things were not looking good. Sure enough, about twenty minutes later, we came across his banged-up canoe floating in some still water. At which point we figured the gators must've got him.

"But just as we're turning back, we heard this faint hootin' and hollerin'. Following the sound, we come across our tourist friend stuck up in an old cypress tree, clinging to the branches for dear life. And circling the tree in the water below him was the biggest alligator I'd ever seen. A monster croc, snaking round and round in the muddy water. And as I live and breathe—this gator was a dirty white from head to tail. It was the legendary Ghost Croc himself! The tourist had found him after all. Or maybe it was the other way around.

"Eager to be the one to bag this remarkable critter, some of the more trigger happy among us began to let loose before we got within range. The Ghost Croc quickly gave up on its snack and, with a flick of his giant tail, sunk out of sight in the dark waters. Then the miserable photographer dropped out of the tree and into our boat, like a ripe apple. He was quite a sight—bright pink from the sun and covered with welts from mosquitoes biting him all night. He was also bleeding badly from a croc bite on his ankle, but he was alive, and he made a full recovery at the local clinic—except for losing his leg below the knee, that is, on account of that bite."

"Ghost Croc, really?" said Ollie, raising a skeptical eyebrow. "And you saw this albino alligator with your own two eyes?"

"As clearly as I see you sitting there," said Herbert. "Better even, as my eyesight was a good deal sharper back then. It's a good thing we didn't give up and call it quits after we found the paddle, or this guy would've ended up a tasty aperitivo for that pale dinosaur."

He had to admit Herbert could really tell a story. But who was he to question his account when he had his own outlandish story that no one believed. Telling his friends earlier had been a mistake. They clearly thought he had a screw loose.

Ollie stood up. "Time for me to go make some flyers."

Herbert walked him out into the hallway, encouraging him to turn the block upside down until he found his cat.

When Ollie pushed open his own front door, he found the apartment still and quiet, just as he had left it. But the old man was right—he shouldn't give up hope. Weren't all cats supposedly born with at least nine get out of jail free cards to use in tight situations? If there was any truth to that at all, then he hoped Pirate still had a few of them left to play.

Pushing up his window for the second time that day, Ollie climbed back outside. The sky was mostly clear, but the sunlight wasn't trickling down to the shaded gardens below. The only movement he noticed were some noisy pigeons strutting about on a ledge.

He stared up at the nearby water tower. Everything was quiet. There were no giant green space turtles out and about at the moment. Another identical water tower stood a little further down on the same roof, which struck Ollie as odd. He examined the distance between him and this neighboring rooftop. It was about thirty feet away, but it was also a couple storeys higher than where he was standing, and it was hard to see how even an acrobatic climber like Pirate could make his way up there. Of course, that space creature could be anywhere right now too.

Ollie was tempted to descend the fire escape to look for Pirate at ground level. But the gardens were chopped up into a collection of mini yards, separated from one another by wooden fences and short brick walls, all of them covered in a tangled mess of leafy vines. He wasn't sure he could climb them, and even if he managed somehow, he knew he wouldn't get very far before some uneasy neighbor called the cops.

11. MRS. BUTLER

[1 p.m.]

here was more activity in the courtyards below than Ollie had realized. Five stories down from his fire escape, and two buildings over to the left, a figure sat tucked away under a green awning, just out of sight from where Ollie had been standing moments ago. She was an elderly lady with steel gray hair pinned up neatly in a bun, and she was sitting quietly at a small wrought iron table sipping tea from a blue-and-white willow pattern cup. Her name was Mrs. Nora Butler, and she was a widow, going on ten years. She had lived in the same one-bedroom ground floor apartment for over thirty years and, as she never tired of telling her nephews, when the time came they were going to have to carry her out of there feet first.

Mrs. Butler had retired nine years earlier from a career as a secretary at a financial firm. She'd been the old-fashioned

kind of secretary who was happy to be in charge of the coffee
and ordering lunch, who could take dictation in shorthand
on a notepad and then type up a letter at a speed of 130 words
a minute, a skill she had learned way back in the day on a
manual typewriter.

But at this stage in her life, she had left all that behind—a
pair of engraved silver candlesticks sitting on her mantelpiece
were the only visible reminders of her career. These days Mrs.
Butler dedicated herself to her true vocation in life—bird-
watching. She was a lifelong member of the Linnean Society
of New York, and, with more time on her hands in retire-
ment, she volunteered her time and skill to Bird Watchers of
America. She had slowly climbed the organization's ranks,
and then a year ago she had been voted in as President of the
New York chapter for a two-year term.

The bureaucracy, the invites, the auctions, the birding
fairs, and the travel to conferences, all of it took up copious
amounts of time and energy. It felt a lot like work, and it was
work, except for the missing paycheck. She realized that her
time might be better spent wandering the park with a pair
of binoculars. But there was some satisfaction to be found in
codifying the rarefied pleasures of the birding world. And of
course she still managed to go on outings with fellow club
members to local parks, and occasionally even upstate. She
had a knack for bird-spotting, and had even made a few
notable sightings herself, including being the first to confirm
a rare painted bunting in Prospect Park a few years back.

She also enjoyed watching birds from the comfort of her
own home. She had two bird feeders set up on her patio. Her
most recent visitors of note were a pair of squawking blue

jays, who seemed to return regularly at this time of year. Just yesterday they had perched themselves right on the edge of her table. She had plucked some raisins from her scone to feed them. They seemed to take a real liking to her. Technically part of the crow family, she'd read that in folklore down south, blue jays were considered servants of the devil. But of course, she had never believed any of that poppycock.

Mrs. Butler's love for birds was matched only by her hatred of cats. She loathed the vicious predatory creatures. They spent their days lying around mooching off their owners, and their nights devastating local wildlife. Her late husband had been fond of cats, a flaw that had always ranked very high on her list of grievances. But she no longer needed to listen to his spirited defense of the cruel creatures, just as she no longer needed to share a bathroom, or a bed. Forty years of marriage had been more than enough for her. Although she concealed it well, her main emotion, on discovering her husband lying motionless on the kitchen floor one afternoon, surrounded by a crumpled and scattered BLT sandwich, was a sudden sense of relief, followed quickly by some thoughts about poetic justice. Live by the sword, die by the sword.

Mrs. Butler sat and sipped her Earl Grey, watching the sparrows flit around her bird feeders. She was keeping an eye out for a pair of mourning doves who were regulars. Even though they were quite common, she still loved seeing their blue eyelids when they blinked, and listening to their soothing coos. She took another small sip of tea, the cup clinking softly as she rested it back on the saucer. She was racking her brain for a solution to the problem that had been vexing her all day, without any luck.

She had thought that trapping the ghastly creature would be the hard part, but it had turned out to be surprisingly easy. A little sprinkled catnip inside the cage and he had walked right in. No, the real problem was how to dispose of the giant cat that was currently sitting in a large coon trap under her dining room table.

She knew she could take the cage over to an animal shelter, and had located a nearby one in the yellow pages. But the truth was she could hardly lift the cage. She had dragged it indoors last night with a supreme effort that had left her with aching arms, gasping for air, and wondering if this was how she was destined to leave this world.

The cat had been a hissing, scratching ball of fury. An enraged demon who had thrown himself every which way inside the cage. She was glad she had ordered a top-of-the-line trap from her garden catalog, as the seething animal had stubbornly tested the cage's strength over and over. Eventually he tired himself out, and just stood crouching, glaring at her with his ears flattened back and whiskers thrust forward. He was a fearsome sight, and even though her bedroom was some distance away from the dining room, the truth was she hadn't slept a wink. He kept hissing periodically all night, and she kept picturing him getting loose and attacking her in her sleep. This was why she needed him gone sooner rather than later.

Her one requirement for disposing of the damned animal was that it be a permanent fix. Normally she would have been quick to put a call in to the super, but she knew the super and his wife owned at least two felines, and she had them pegged as sympathizers. The last thing she needed was to be subjected to their horrified looks and have them track down the cat's owner to return him. She knew quite well where the cat originated from already, as she had watched the young man and his cat cavorting on his fire escape on several occasions through the lenses of her ten-by-forty-two Nikon binoculars.

But even if she managed to somehow throw the caged beast in the trunk of a cab and get down to a shelter, who could say that the shelter folks wouldn't also figure out how to reunite the hellish creature with his owner. These days cats all had those darn tracking chips. She just didn't think she could chance it.

That left her to figure out how to get rid of the damn thing on her own. The cage was too wide to fit in her bathtub. She knew this because she had measured. She had already tried throwing a garbage bag over the cage, but the cat's claws had reached through the bars and ripped the bag to shreds in mere seconds.

Mrs. Butler was originally from Tennessee, and her great grandfather had been a colonel in the Civil War. It was a part of her family's heritage that she was particularly proud of. She had several mementos of his from the war that she treasured, including a saber that was hanging on her living room wall.

Living in New York, she'd had to tamp down her southern pride, as people here just didn't understand that sort of thing. But honor, tradition, and courage still meant something in her family. They were the values that she'd clung to her whole life. When faced with a predicament, she often stopped to ask herself what Colonel Blake would do in her place. She pictured him now, standing proudly before her in full confederate uniform, his mustache billowing in the breeze and his eyes blazing, full of fury and passion. Her mental image of him was so real she felt like she could almost reach out and touch him.

"What are you doing sitting there drinking tea? Grab my sword and run the damn beast through!" he yelled. And then he spun around and faded to nothingness as he stormed away. She was alone again with her thoughts. And while a part of her was itching to just grab the cutlass and make her ancestor proud, she worried that, even if she succeeded, it would make an awful mess on her carpet. No, there had to be another way.

She took another sip of her now lukewarm tea, disappointed that nothing but sparrows had shown at the feeders. Suddenly, an idea came to her. The blasted creature must be getting hungry, she reasoned. So maybe she should pop over to the supermarket and pick up some cat food? And then she could stop at the hardware store on the way home and buy some rat poison.

This plan had a nice simplicity to it. Of course, it would be much easier to just make the call to animal control and see if someone would come and take him away. She could tell them she suspected rabies. Maybe smear some baking soda around his muzzle, and hope they did the dirty work for her? Which path should she take? It was a conundrum. She stared down at the dregs of her now empty cup.

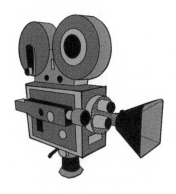

12. CASSANDRA

[1:15 p.m.]

C assandra Bell had a sizable telescope planted by her living room window. It was her dad's telescope really, from back in his school days when he was still living in New York. She had dragged it out of the basement storage area and put it to use for the popular New York pastime of spying on her neighbors.

At the moment the lens was trained on the gray-haired lady sitting in the courtyard across the way. Cassandra was squinting into the viewfinder, watching her drink tea, which was not terribly exciting. Still, after last night, she had some burning questions about this woman: Cassandra had been dozing on the couch in front of the TV when she'd been woken up around quarter to twelve by some piercing yowls. Rushing over to the open window she arrived just in time to witness a strange scene. A light went on in the old lady's courtyard, followed by the old woman herself bursting out of her backdoor, dressed in a long black nightgown, and with pink rollers in her hair. The woman rushed over to the bushes and dragged an enormous cage, with a large, screeching animal in it, back toward her doorway.

Cassandra had the telescope aimed at her in a flash and just managed to get the thing focused before the back door swung shut. Inside the cage, she'd glimpsed a swirling, angry ball of fur that had stood still for just a split second. Long enough for her to recognize a huge black-and-white cat. A cat she'd delighted in watching many times in the gardens below. Cassandra was shocked—the old lady had gone and trapped the poor animal.

Infuriated, she'd grabbed a phone and dialed 9-1-1. Despite her protests, the operator had transferred her to animal control. There, a patient individual explained that it was not illegal to trap an animal on your own property, and that, unless the animal was reported as abused or rabid, they didn't have the resources to get involved. He even hinted that this neighbor might be doing the cat a favor, and would likely take the animal to a shelter where it would be better cared for or adopted.

What Cassandra couldn't get the guy on the other end of the line to understand was the maniacal look in the old lady's eyes as she'd slammed her door shut. She did not look like any do-gooder Cassandra had ever seen. Even now, as Cassandra watched her calmly taking another sip of tea, she could swear that the old lady was plotting something nefarious. *I wonder what you're up to, you old bat. Nothing good, I'll bet.*

Unfortunately, Cassandra couldn't stand there watching

the woman drink tea all day. She needed to finish getting ready. She had an audition to go to for a national snack food commercial. It was a big opportunity, though she wouldn't let herself get her hopes up. She was an audition veteran of eight months now, and she knew how rarely these things panned out. Rarely meaning basically never. At least not for her yet.

Cassandra put the finishing touches on her makeup in front of the bathroom mirror, lit by a ring of yellow globe lights. They always wanted a natural look, so she was careful not to overdo it with mascara, and she chose an understated peach shade for her lips. She'd blown out her hair already to give it some body, and the chestnut locks cascaded around her face, complementing the green sundress she was wearing. A dress that she practically lived in these days. She knew what they were looking for—they wanted the girl-next-door look, only bustier and better looking. And with a little help from the right bra, she would fit the bill nicely.

Of course, when Cassandra looked into the mirror, she always zeroed in on her flaws. She'd clearly been standing in the wrong line when they were handing out plump round lips. But what bothered her most was being slightly cross-eyed. A mild case of strabismus is how her family doctor put it. Her depth perception wasn't the best, and she had to be careful going down stairs, but it didn't affect her otherwise. Except when scrutinizing casting directors demanded that she look straight into the camera.

She made a pouty face and gave herself a critical once over. She needed to look like she was glowing, even when she was working on four hours of sleep, stressed about the call back, and had forgotten to eat lunch. If she could book this commercial, she could coast off the paycheck for the next six months.

The phone rang as she was shoving her heels into her tote bag. She knew it would be her dad. He called her at least twice a day, usually at the worst possible times. He was not adjusting well to his only child moving three thousand miles away to live by herself in New York. It had always been just the two of them ever since her mom died when Cassandra was just seven. She picked up the receiver in the kitchen.

As she'd suspected, her father quickly asked her if she'd had any luck finding a roommate yet. She told him she hadn't, but promised, yet again, to find someone soon. Then she explained she was running late and hung up.

Her dad had inherited this apartment from his aunt when she'd passed away many years ago, so technically he was now her landlord. She'd managed to put off the whole roommate thing while she'd supervised a much-needed remodeling, but with construction over, her time was up.

She'd enjoyed playing interior decorator. She'd transformed the place from a beige bourgeois nightmare into a stylish bohemian pad. Perfect for a soon-to-be starlet. The Moroccan mirror she'd hung above the nonworking fireplace had been an inspired choice. But her biggest coup was a large bronze Ganesh statue that she had picked up for just fifty bucks at a street fair, and was now the new centerpiece in the entryway. The Hindu deity was known as the remover of obstacles, and he brought amazing energy to the space.

Her dad did not agree. He had flipped when he'd caught sight of the Ganesh statue on his recent visit. "Good lord!

What is this hideous, hippy claptrap?" he'd protested. She had drawn him away into the living room and then distracted him by whipping out a gag gift she'd found in a novelty store. It was an alien detector gizmo that scanned the surroundings for anomalies using a magnetometer. The joke being that it would alert people to any passing UFOs. Her dad was an astrophysicist for SETI back in the Bay Area, so he'd gotten a real kick out of it, explaining gleefully that it was a perfect example of the kind of junk science that alien abduction fanatics subscribed to.

She was using the device as a bookend for her science fiction bookshelf. She was a huge sci-fi geek, just like her dad, and she had an extensive collection of books and movies featuring strange creatures from outer space. It was the family business after all. The detector lit up with a green light when you pushed the button and was a fun conversation piece. But they were never able to get any other responses from it, and they'd soon concluded the purple light feature was defective.

Until about three weeks ago, that is, when she'd been woken up one night by a loud beeping that she'd thought at first was the fire alarm. Tracing the sound, she was astonished to discover that the UFO detector was to blame and that it was also flashing with a bright purple light. She'd had to remove the batteries from the darn thing because she couldn't figure out any other way to shut it up.

When she'd told her dad about it the next day, he had cracked up, teasingly suggesting that she'd better keep her eyes peeled for little green men. "I thought that was your job?" she'd said. He'd found her joke less funny because as much as he loved to poke fun at Area 51 type conspiracies, he took his own work very seriously. Her father and his colleagues all shared a deep conviction that intelligent life was out there, somewhere in the universe, waiting to be discovered. For herself, Cassandra wasn't so sure. She was more in the I'll-believe-it-when-I-see-it—camp.

13. AXZLEPROVA

[1:15 p.m.]

■ n the past few weeks, AxzleProva had observed a wide
■ variety of Earth cats from their rooftop post. Cats were a
common sight in many windows, and a substantial number
of them appeared at night on the streets below. Their most
notable subject was a large black-and-white cat who appeared
every evening in the trees and patios on the garden side. He
proved to be an impressive and resourceful specimen.

Even Prova had been forced to admit that, based on his
bold and gregarious temperament, he was a highly promising
first contact possibility. Whenever he had popped up on their
thermographic scanners, they'd made detailed recordings of
his movements and behavior, hoping that sooner or later he
would find his way a bit closer to their ship.

But it was not to be. Last night, they were alarmed to
discover they were not the only ones tracking this cat. They

had watched in horror as their subject had been lured into a metal cage through the use of scented bait. They'd trained their scopes on the old human female who had set the trap. She had demonstrated classic signs of interspecies aggression. Although they were not there to study humans, they were in agreement that this was yet more anecdotal evidence of homo sapiens' problematic outlook on life. They'd sat for hours in the ship's plush command chair, debating the best way forward for their mission. Exhausted, they'd eventually let the matter rest and took turns sleeping during the early morning hours. And then the disastrous pigeon incident had interrupted their breakfast.

Now, with the Earth's singular sun just past its zenith, their fears of being discovered were beginning to die down. But Prova still hadn't forgiven her partner for his rash ploy earlier that day. And he hadn't given up on trying to lure her back into conversation.

"Prova, why don't we do something to help that poor creature?" Axzle asked.

You know full well that intervening in any manner is against regulations. Her words appeared on the main screen for him to read. *It's frustrating, I know. He was our most favorable research subject . . .*

"But, it's . . . criminal!" Axzle shot back, interrupting her before she could finish typing.

There is nothing we can do, Prova replied calmly. Axzle shot her a dirty look and his face dropped into a sulk. His attitude reminded Prova of an ill-tempered school turtle. Once again, she was thankful that they had agreed not to activate the telepathic link system. Sometimes it was better to just keep your own thoughts to yourself.

Interspecies violence was frowned upon back in the Amalgamation. It was only overlooked when it took place within the context of feeding. But Prova knew it was unlikely the old lady considered the captive cat a food resource. There had been no observed examples of cats being consumed by humans for nourishment in this corner of the planet. Clearly cats had trained the locals to think of such a practice as completely out of bounds.

A frustrated Axzle renewed his arguments to step in and free the cat. He suggested that under Amalgamation rules, they could justify intervening if they could prove the cat was both an advanced sentient being and in mortal danger. Prova inconveniently pointed out that they weren't sure of either fact and flat out refused to go along. It was as if he had completely forgotten that they had been spotted by a human earlier that day.

Prova was just as crestfallen over the capture of the promising feline subject as he was. After all, it practically meant starting their research over from scratch. But she didn't think Axzle appreciated the risks involved in their assignment. Even though they had gone through the same training, he was too optimistic by nature to give much thought to the danger they were in. They were utterly surrounded by millions of these primitive Earthlings. Creatures who lacked either scales or proper fur, their hide reminding Prova of the giant burrowing worms on their home planet. And the strange affinity they had for covering their bare skin with ridiculous trappings only made them more repulsive. The field manual detailed various cases where field operatives had fallen into the hands of natives while on assignments on various planets, and they were uniformly unpleasant. Prova knew that detection and capture by these hairless apes would almost certainly result in them being experimented on in deplorable ways.

14. MANOLO

[2 p.m.]

Traffic was barely inching along on Houston Street. Frustrated drivers took turns leaning on their horns, to no effect. Manolo was waiting for his sister outside the Second Avenue F subway stop at Allen Street. He'd telephoned her earlier, and she had agreed to meet him after lunch, promising to introduce him to a friend of hers who was adept at handling difficult personal problems.

He watched people stream up the subway stairs in waves, keeping an eye open among the stragglers for his sister's familiar silhouette. Like him, she was heavyset, with curly brown hair. But Maricela had always carried herself differently, with her chin tilted up. This had earned her the nickname "la Princesa" growing up. If Manolo had done reasonably well in life, then by comparison Maricela was a superstar. She had graduated from college, and had made a successful career for herself at a book publisher. Manolo's heart swelled with pride when he thought about how far she'd come.

Manolo rarely got to see her these days. Not just because they lived in different boroughs, but because the two women in his life detested each other. Natalya resented how close he was to his sister, while Maricela felt that Manolo had made a bad match.

Manolo finally caught sight of his sister trudging slowly up the subway steps. She was wearing a simple gray cotton dress, accented with a chunky pearl necklace. Her face lit up when she saw him, and they exchanged double cheek kisses and a hug. Manolo found himself beaming adoringly into his sister's eyes.

"God, I've missed seeing you, Princesa. You're lookin' great. Thanks for meeting me."

"It's good to see you too Manny. I wish it hadn't been so long."

"Yeah, me too, but you know how it is—I don't have time to catch a train to Queens these days."

"I know. Who would've guessed you'd turn into such a Manhattan snob?"

"Now you know that's not true!" he protested vigorously.

"Do I? God forbid you head out to another borough and check on your only sister once in a while," she said huffily.

Manolo frowned. "Look, I know. I need to come out and see you more often. But convincing Natalya to head out to Queens ain't easy."

"Then leave her behind, doesn't matter to me. Speaking of the devil, how is Natalya these days?"

"She's good. Same as always."

"Busy making your life a living hell?"

"Hey, I know she's not your favorite person, but she's my wife, so lay off."

"You always were a loyal son of a bitch," she said with a chuckle. "But we should be able to talk about these things."

"What's the point in talking about things that can't be fixed."

Maricela was silent for a moment as she led the way east. Then she spoke up hesitantly. "Actually, since you mention it, I was thinking that if you are going to ask a favor from the Lady of the Shadows, you might as well forget about this roof nonsense and make it something worthwhile."

"Maricela, try to understand, this roof nonsense as you call it is driving me nuts."

"I'm getting that impression," she said, looking at him with concern. "But, hey, why don't we make it a twofer then? One offering for this roof business, and another bigger one for your . . . relationship?"

"Offering?"

"C'mon, Manny, I told you on the phone, you've got to leave something for Santa Muerte. And don't think you can get away with dropping a cheap pack of cigarettes at her feet. You're going to have to spring for a bead necklace and a large candle. Maybe throw in some flowers for good measure."

"How much we talking?"

"Maybe thirty bucks? I don't know. Don't get cheap on me." She glared at him.

"Don't worry, I brought cash." Manolo had suspected this Santa Muerte business would run to money. Which was tricky since Natalya kept a tight grip on his wallet. Luckily he had a little emergency fund stashed away in a basement nook that Natalya knew nothing about. Small bills from tenant tips he'd neglected to mention to her.

"I'm surprised Natalya was on board with this little excursion," Maricela said.

"She doesn't know. She thinks I'm at the hardware store. And let's make sure we keep it that way."

"Got it," said Maricela with a conspiratorial smile.

"So this friend of yours—Rosa—she works at a botanica?"

"She's the owner," said Maricela. "She's just the person to talk to about unusual problems like yours. And she has a small Santa Muerte altar in the back of her store."

"You're gonna enjoy this aren't you. Watching me spend my hard-earned cash on this baloney."

"Yeah, I'm gonna love this."

They walked a ways in silence while Manolo thought over his sister's suggestion. It occurred to him that if he was already getting himself involved in this Santa Muerte business, it couldn't hurt to ask for a little improvement on the home-front too.

"I guess I can get on board with asking Santa Muerte for some help with Natalya. But there's no way I'm casting a curse on my wife, let me be clear about that."

"Who said anything about a curse? Don't be so dramatic. Besides, just because you have a demon in human form curling up in bed next to you every night is no reason to stoop to dark magic. Just light a candle for love and ask Santa Muerte to smooth off Natalya's hard edges a little." She flashed her familiar impish smile.

"I forgot how funny you are," Manolo said irritably. He felt foolish going through with this whole procedure. And guilty too—was he betraying his religion? "This had better work," he muttered under his breath.

15. NATALYA

[2 p.m.]

Natalya had been watching Manolo's increasingly erratic behavior for the past few weeks with a mixture of curiosity and amusement. After being married for three years, she felt entitled to the perverse pleasure she got from her husband's minor miseries. If she was stuck being married to an imbecile, she might as well get some enjoyment out of it—that was how she saw it.

She'd realized her tragic mistake after only the first few months of marriage when it dawned on her that her husband had no real ambition. He'd already found his level, and he was content to spend the rest of his days in this dirty little world. She considered this unforgivable, since it meant that she, too, would share this fate. And he was too stupid to even get that. But if he had been smarter, he wouldn't be killing himself to keep this dump going in the first place.

With his experience, and a new suit, he could easily apply for a super position at a Park Avenue building, or one of those new luxury condos sprouting up all over the place. But no, the pitiful moron was perfectly satisfied unclogging toilets and sweeping floors in this crumbling cesspool.

Still, she'd stuck it out with him for the past few years, putting up with disappointment after disappointment. At least Manolo had one saving quality—he took direction well. Maybe two, if you counted his frequent apologizing. Which she didn't.

Natalya knew she had let this situation, whatever it was, go on for too long. And now he had turned to that crazy sister of his for help. Did Manolo really think she wouldn't find out? Didn't he realize by now that his mind was like a transparent fishbowl to her? That she could anticipate all his little goldfish thoughts before they even popped into his fat, sweaty head?

She had to admit, she was perplexed this time as to the source of her husband's misery. Which hadn't mattered a lot until now. But she'd managed to gather a few clues from the rambling he did in his sleep—the man was like a radio, broadcasting all his problems nightly to whoever tuned in to listen. From what she'd put together so far, she knew it had something to do with the roof. There was something going on up on the roof that was making him crazy.

Natalya had no idea what this could be. Some tenant growing marijuana? Nude sunbathers? She felt like anything was possible in this place. Their building was a magnet for crackpots who were constantly finding new ways to make trouble. Only last night, the kooky old lady in 1A had caused some sort of ruckus in her yard, and when they had rung her doorbell, she had told them to go away. Some nerve that old witch had, waking up half the neighborhood and then pretending like nothing had happened.

Natalya shifted her grip on the mop she was holding as she exited the elevator on the ninth floor. She turned left and walked over to the stairwell, where she stopped. *Why have I come here,* she wondered. Her mind had gone blank. She twirled around in a small circle trying to get her bearings. *I have no business on the roof,* she realized abruptly.

Natalya grabbed a hold of herself, let out a deep breath, and shook herself like a dog. She wasn't sure what was going on, but she came from a long line of Ukrainian farmers who prided themselves on nothing if not sheer single-mindedness. Once they set themselves to a task, they would see it through tenaciously, no matter what. She wasn't sure exactly why, but deep down in her core, she knew that she had come here to go up to the roof, and she resolved that nothing on Earth, or in the heavens above, was going to stop her from doing just that.

With great difficulty, she placed one foot on the stairs, and then the next. Making progress bit by bit, she soon rounded the bend in the stairs. Above her, a grimy skylight let in a faint glow of daylight. Here she hit another snag, as some part of her mind insisted she had not brought the right key. But she focused her thoughts carefully. I don't need a key, she reminded herself—the roof is never locked. The two conflicting notions duked it out for a moment, and then she continued on her way. Reaching the top step, she reached out and pressed the bar across the exit, then she gave the door a swift kick. It swung open before her with a loud clang.

16. AXZLEPROVA

[2 p.m.]

The alarm sensors were blaring once more in AxzlePro-va's command station. They exchanged looks. Their first glance was to the exterior camera, which showed that the top of the ship was clear of birds. Based on the triggers that had been tripped, it seemed that this threat was approaching from the building's interior. Something, or someone, was breaking past their blockades.

AxzleProva had taken numerous steps to prevent such an incursion, setting wards and psychological blocks at various possible entry points to the roof. Humans, like many social species, were considered highly suggestible and easily distracted, so a combination of rudimentary cognitive redirection devices typically worked well at keeping them away.

The fact that someone had overcome these obstacles was

a troubling sign. Prova quickly put away her half-finished snack while Axzle grabbed the stun-blaster from its compartment and powered it up. She shot him a nasty look, and Axzle just shrugged in reply.

"Don't worry. It's just a precaution. I'll set it to immobilize."

"I don't believe a word you say anymore," Prova replied, before catching herself and putting a hand to her mouth.

"You do realize that we may have to communicate verbally to prevent our mission from becoming jeopardized, right? I don't have time to read your silly notes."

Prova was about to respond furiously when the door to the roof flew open and a figure appeared on their screen. A blond human female, holding a weapon of some sort. Wait, on closer inspection, it looked like a cleaning instrument. Still, they couldn't take any chances. Prova exchanged alarmed looks with her shell-mate.

"Let's just sit tight and hope she doesn't discover our ship," Axzle whispered. Prova nodded.

They watched the woman make the rounds on the roof. She looked as if she was searching for something, and her expression was one of grim determination. For a few minutes, it seemed that their camouflaged ship was going to pass this close-up test with flying colors, and then the woman turned and stared up at the water tower that was their vessel.

They watched aghast as she set down her mop, and grabbed hold of the ladder leading up the side of their ship.

"Just follow my lead," Axzle said stonily.

Prova looked at him warily, but without the hostility she'd been showing only moments before. They both knew that, like it or not, they were partners in this situation. The only way to get through this was to work together.

"Just don't do anything stupid," she whispered to him.

17. NATALYA

[2:15 p.m.]

With a tight grip on her mop, Natalya stepped through the open door into the afternoon light. The aluminum-coated rooftop glistened before her, and on first inspection seemed quite deserted. It looked no different than the dozens of other times she'd been up here. But the more she poked around, the more convinced she became that something was out of place. She walked slowly along the roof's perimeter to make sure there was nothing suspicious tucked away in some hidden corner. It was a large rooftop, and it took her a few minutes to trace the length and breadth of the giant E shape, but she found nothing out of the ordinary.

She ended up back in the center of the roof, where she stood looking around distrustfully. Something looked different up here, but whatever it was still escaped her. She was staring absently into space when the second water tower came into sharp focus, and it suddenly clicked. There were two water towers looming over her, when she knew the building had only ever had one.

"That's impossible," she said out loud to herself, furrowing her pretty eyebrows and pressing a finger to her lips as she stared skeptically at this other tower.

She walked up to the structure and put a hand on one of the legs. It felt cold and solid and very real, yet she knew it shouldn't even be there. She was the super's wife, after all. She was pretty much the brains of the operation, and there was simply no way a new tower could have been installed on the roof without her knowledge.

It looked just like the other one. But her instincts told her there was something odd about it. For a moment, she considered heading downstairs and waiting for Manolo to return from wherever he had disappeared to so she could hear what he had to say about it. But in the end, she was too curious and wanted to scope things out herself. Otherwise, she risked looking like a fool when they called the landlord later on. In a small corner of her brain, a little alarm bell was going off, but she simply ignored it.

Natalya set down her mop, took a firm hold of the tower's narrow ladder, and, propelled by the vague suspicion that the large container above her might not be filled with water, began her climb.

She made her way up with steadfast resolve and soon reached the side of the barrel. Here, she was surprised to see part of the tower's siding unexpectedly slide open. She had no time at all to react when three green arms reached out from the hatch, and pulled her toward the tower's interior. She clung to the ladder with all her might, but they soon overpowered her and yanked her inside.

She landed facedown on a rubbery floor. Terrified, she flipped herself over. Her eyes took a moment to adjust to the darkened interior, and when they did, she found herself facing a two-headed creature beyond her wildest imaginings. Her eyes bulged out of their sockets.

The creature made a chirping sound and a croaking English voice emerged from a speaker somewhere. "Do not be alarmed," it said.

"What the hell are you!" she screamed.

Desperate, she tried to climb to her feet so she could escape but found herself unable to do anything other than wiggle her arms and legs as a mysterious glowing force had enveloped her. The alien approached her slowly, a metallic instrument in one of its four hands.

More chirping from one of the two heads. "Resistance is useless," it declared in the same throaty tone as before. However this statement was intended, it only served to terrify her further. Her mouth opened wide, and she let out a piercing scream. The monster pressed the tip of the device to her upper arm and she felt a sharp jab, like a needle prick. The effect of the drug was instantaneous—her eyes fluttered closed and she slumped down to the floor, unconscious.

18. CONSTANCE

[2 p.m.]

C onstance Frizzler double locked her door and plodded up the stairs. The building was always quiet at midday, which suited her just fine. Rounding the bend on the sixth floor, she paused near 6C and listened. She knew that Oliver was one of the few neighbors to find his way regularly to the roof. But typically not until much later in the day. She didn't need that nitwit poking around while she was sunbathing on the roof.

Constance was wearing her pink terry cloth robe and matching slippers. Practical and comfortable, she always slipped into her robe whenever she was home. She even had a spare hanging in her closet, just in case breakfast jam or rabbit pee made a wardrobe change necessary.

The roof door was never locked. Constance pushed it open and stepped out of the dingy stairwell into the bright autumn sun. She plucked her heart-shaped sunglasses from her forehead and settled them snugly on her face. Her folded lounge chair was leaning against the wall right where she'd left it. Extending it, she lined it up with the sun and plopped herself down with a satisfied grunt.

Court wasn't in session today, so she had the whole day off. Thank god. Everyone thought a court reporter's job was so quaint. They didn't understand that you had to be able to type 225 words a minute, with 95 percent accuracy. And you had to read off your shorthand transcript at a moment's notice when the judge demanded it. Constance considered herself competent in her chosen profession, but she was worried her days in court were numbered. The city had begun to replace stenographers with electronic recording devices. Constance wished them luck trying to read back testimony when someone inevitably forgot to turn the damn recorder on. She'd heard that'd happened recently in a big case and they'd had to redo the whole day's proceedings. Not exactly a cost savings when that happened, was it?

Constance settled a little deeper into the lounge chair, the plastic slats giving way to the contours of her backside. She slid a white leg out from the confines of the robe and let the neckline drop open. So far, October had coughed up a fair amount of sunny weather. But winter was around the corner with its short and cloudy days. Better not to think about it.

Constance loved the sunshine almost as much as she hated tan lines. But it was a delicate business—lying out in a string bikini on her East Village rooftop. Thankfully running into anyone up here was a rare occurrence.

She was concealed on her right by the roof's entryway hut. But from other angles, she was in plain view. She liked to keep an eye on the windows of the tallish building on Avenue A. The occupants of its upper floors had an unobstructed view of her roof. Of course, it was also possible that some pervert in a distant high-rise might watch her through a telescope. Nothing she could do about that. Heck, for all she knew there might even be a satellite in space snapping pictures of her at this very moment.

Technically she wasn't supposed to be up here at all. If the super caught her up on the roof, she was prepared to plead ignorance to the rules. Plausible deniability. She hadn't sat in on over a decades worth of criminal cases without learning a thing or two. Constance tugged slowly on the end of her belt until it slipped free of the knot, luxuriating in the feel of the warm rays on her bare skin. The sunshine was revitalizing, and that was something she sorely needed.

She was beyond tired these days. Not to mention stressed out, strung out, and perhaps even a little unhinged. Besides the usual pressures of work, she now had a rabbit problem to deal with. Unbelievably, the damned pet store had sold her a pregnant rabbit. It'd been quite a surprise for her when she'd arrived home the other day to find six unexpected baby bunnies waiting for her. Bringing the total number of rabbits currently in her apartment to double digits.

A part of her had been elated by the sudden appearance of the tiny bunnies. But there was no denying it was a problem. The pet store had refused to accept any responsibility and wished her luck, pointing out that new rabbits could start breeding as early as ten weeks of age. Constance wasn't sure what the ideal number of rabbits was for her living space, but it had been crowded enough with four rabbits.

It was fundamentally a math problem. How many cubic liters of living space did you need per bunny? A math problem, wrapped in a bunny problem, wrapped in a sanity problem. Constance was a seasoned New Yorker, and she knew that it was silly little things like this that could send your life in this city into a downward spiral. If the superintendent got one whiff of the budding rabbit colony in her apartment, there'd be an eviction notice posted on her door before she could say Bugs Bunny. And then what would she do? Rents had shot up everywhere in Manhattan. Even a little shoebox like her apartment was barely affordable.

When she'd first arrived in the city twelve years ago, the exorbitant costs had felt like a reasonable trade-off for all the glamour and excitement. But not anymore—the scales had well and truly fallen from her eyes. If you were surrounded by friends, the city's faults were easy to overlook. But one by one, her friends had all drifted away, moving on to some other stage in their lives. But not her. She was the last one, all alone, at an age when it was hard to meet new people.

She'd done her best to strike up new friendships, but most people seemed to find her quite humorless these days. Which in turn only made her more embittered about life. And so with each passing year, her resemblance to her infamous Aunt Matilda grew stronger. She was afraid she would wake up one day and find herself transformed into a cranky old lady who everyone hated. It seemed practically inevitable.

Constance decided she wasn't going to let her bleak thoughts ruin her sunbath. What she needed was a little pick-me-up to boost her mood. Luckily she had come prepared. She pulled a bottle of Jose Cuervo from the deep pocket of her robe and unscrewed the cap. She tipped a splash of the golden liquid into a shot glass she'd stashed in her other pocket and, placing the bottle down on the ground beside her, she tossed the warm liquid back in a practiced motion. She was aware it was early in the day to get started. But it was her day off, and she was determined to let her hair down a little.

Most days she had to pass as the mousy, buttoned-down woman that the court expected her to be. She didn't know how much longer she could keep up that pretense. She had wild fantasies where she chucked it all and made a break for it. She imagined herself giving the trial judge the finger and running out of the courtroom chased by court officers as he held her in contempt.

Her professionalism, her patience, and her manners had all run dry. It was as if a spring inside her had been wound tighter and tighter until one day, it just snapped. After that, she had started muttering to herself in public. She was embarrassed when she caught herself doing this, but it happened now with increasing frequency. When a thought came to her with a red-hot urgent sticker slapped on it, she just had to think it out loud. Blurt it out to the world. And anyone who happened to overhear would look at her suspiciously.

The sound of voices carrying from somewhere nearby spooked her, and she whisked her robe closed. She hoped it wasn't young Oliver banging about. If his head poked up the ladder when she was flipped on her stomach, he was bound to get an eyeful. A silent minute went by, and Constance let herself relax once more.

These were the risks an urban sunbather had to contend with. But it was worth it if it added a little touch of color to her pasty complexion. Constance liked to stand in her underwear in front of her closet mirror every night, carefully appraising her skin and her figure. She was satisfied that she still looked good for her age, in spite of a few gray hairs and her curves becoming a little more pronounced.

Not that anyone noticed her looks these days. She'd become invisible to men somehow. She sometimes wondered what would happen if she stepped into the path of a good-looking guy on the street. Would he just walk right through her like a ghost? The truth was she had never rebounded after getting dumped by her last boyfriend, seven long years ago. Her dating life had gone into free fall, plummeting to the pavement below, where it had gone—splat.

Perhaps it was time to start dating older men. But she just wasn't ready for that yet. She might never be ready. Her patience for men had always been limited to begin with, so she doubted she could make it work with a fat, balding representative of the species.

Constance debated whether a second shot of tequila was a wise notion. She decided it was much too soon. Right on the heels of the first, really. But she poured herself one anyway and sent it on its merry way.

Constance added up the negatives in her mind—unloved, invisible, borderline alcoholic. And crazy, she couldn't forget about that. Even her own mother, disappointed in how she'd turned out, barely remembered to call on her birthday anymore.

A strange shimmer on the rooftop of the suspect

building on Avenue A snapped Constance out of her depressing thoughts. She quickly whipped her robe closed and knotted the sash. Could it be a camera? New York photographers with their zoom lenses were such a menace.

But no, it wasn't a photographer at all. There was a woman climbing the nearby water tower. It was her silver pendant earrings that were catching the light. This woman looked out of place. She had long hair and was dressed fashionably in tight jeans that hugged her hips and a white blouse that had not been designed for maintenance work. Constance watched her curiously as she went up, one ladder rung at a time.

She soon made it to the barrel of the tower, and then something much stranger happened. A panel slid open on the water tower and four green skinny arms stretched out and grabbed hold of the woman. She clung desperately to the ladder for a moment but was soon overpowered and yanked into the interior, letting out a loud yelp. The panel slid shut, and everything was silent once more. It had all happened in a matter of moments. Constance barely had time to sit up straight in her chair. But she'd gotten a good look at those arms. They were long, and round, and they bent in all the wrong places. Not to mention the lime-like color and fine, lizard-like scales. Whatever creature these arms belonged to was not human. She had peered into the shadowy interior of the tower and made out a dimly round shape with two heads balanced on long necks. Four yellow alien eyes had glowed in the darkness, staring out at their prey.

Moments later, Constance heard a muffled scream coming from the direction of the tower. She knew New York was a city where unexpected and sometimes bizarre oddities lurked around every corner. But even by New York standards, this was completely off the charts. What the whole thing had looked like, from start to finish, was an alien abduction. Yes, unmistakably so—an alien abduction.

Constance glanced down at the empty glass at her side, and then back up at the roof. Had someone spiked her booze? It didn't make any sense. Normally two shots was barely enough for her to get a little buzz going.

It was almost as if she was experiencing a total break from reality.

Was it possible that after years of taking little baby steps, she had finally flipped her lid? An extraterrestrial hiding on a rooftop in the middle of New York? Who was she kidding? It was unthinkable. There was only one plausible explanation, and it was that she had lost her freakin' marbles. No ifs, ands, or buts about it. She had always seen herself succumbing to a slow and steady decline. But instead it was as if her sanity had been slammed into by a truck.

Constance took a deep breath and leaned back in her chair. She was mad at herself for never taking a vacation. There was a reason people dragged themselves to the Jersey shore once a year. Something about sticking your toes in the sand and listening to the waves functioned as a mental reset button, immunizing people to another year of mundane tasks and minor indignities. But she'd always scoffed at going to the shore.

The booze probably deserved a share of the blame. Even her darling rabbits were probably a factor. She'd allowed herself to be carried along by a river of tequila and rabbits, and had earned herself room and board at the closest nuthouse.

Constance took a series of deep breaths as she stared up at the water tower. Slowly, the initial shock began to subside.

"It is what it is. I'm nutty as a fruitcake, that's all," she exclaimed out loud.

A strange sense of relief washed over her. Now that she had accepted her newfound status as a lunatic, first class, all the pressure she'd been under to hold herself together was melting away. It dawned on her that from now on, she could just be her own crazy self and not worry so much about the repercussions. At last she could just live her life unapologetically. At least, that is, until the day they came to drag her away.

Having accepted her fate, she wondered if there was any reason to deny herself a third shot of tequila. It hardly seemed to matter anymore. She downed another glass, shook off her robe, and stretched out her limbs, no longer caring if anyone saw her in her skimpy bikini. She closed her eyes, luxuriating in the warmth of the sun, a hesitant smile on her face.

Perhaps it was best to turn the whole thing on its head and think of this as a red-letter day. "How should I celebrate my new life as a madwoman?" Constance asked herself out loud.

It came to her in a flash. Last Halloween she had purchased an adult-sized bunny costume. It was basically a pink hoodie with eyes and ears, matching sweatpants, and slippers. She hadn't picked up the costume for a costume party or anything like that—no one invited her to parties anymore. No, the holiday had just given her a good excuse to walk up to the register with the plush outfit in her hands without embarrassment. She wore it a few times a week when she was home alone, with the blinds drawn. She would sit on her couch and spend some quality time with her bunnies. She didn't know why, but wearing the rabbit costume made her happy.

She had always been ashamed, as well as fearful that someone would discover her secret. But no more. The time had come to introduce the world to bunny Constance. People were always saying she was no fun. Well she would show them exactly how much fun she could be. From now on, she would grab life by the bunny ears.

19. ROGER

[11 a.m.–3 p.m.]

Roger Grant found himself unable to put a good spin on things lately. Somewhere along the line, his life had gone off the rails. There was simply no denying it. He was in his late thirties and still living at home with his mother. He'd recently settled for a minimum wage job at the Sweet Dreams Mattress Warehouse in Union Square, which had felt like hitting rock bottom. But a few months into his new job, Roger realized he would need to revise his notion of rock bottom. Business at the mattress store was down. The manager was under a lot of pressure, and one of his new initiatives had been to demote Roger from sales person on the floor to person standing outside the store all day, holding a sign advertising mattress discounts. In answer to Roger's weather related inquiry, he'd been informed that he shouldn't let a little light rain interfere with his duties.

After weighing his options, and realizing he had none, Roger had swallowed his pride and reluctantly assumed his new post. He had parked himself outside the store, with his 30-percent-off sign, and done his best to wave people in the direction of the mattress store doors, hoping that no one from his school days would walk by and recognize him. He consoled himself with the notion that things simply couldn't get any worse. But once again, his own lack of imagination betrayed him. Because when Roger and his sign failed to improve the bottom line, his boss hit on the brilliant idea that what Roger needed was some kind of eye-catching costume. He left the details of the actual design and execution to Roger, so long as it was cheap, theatrical, and related in some way to mattresses. Roger had politely asked if he would be expected to wear this costume in public. His boss had replied: "Exactly! Now you're getting it!"

Needless to say, Roger had very nearly quit on the spot, but he shrewdly decided to take his time putting the costume together first. This ploy would buy him a little time to line up another job. Maybe his anthropology degree, from a reputable institution, mind you, would impress the manager of a coffee shop somewhere?

Roger purchased a shiny sky blue jumpsuit from a nearby costume store, as well as a carton of large cotton balls and some fabric glue. He proceeded to painstakingly glue the fluffy white balls to the jumpsuit, coating them in hairspray first to give them cohesion. He performed this delicate task in the backroom area of the mattress store, taking his sweet time and ignoring his boss's requests that he put it in gear. Somehow he didn't think his manager would have an easy time finding anyone else who was willing to sacrifice their dignity by wearing this suit. Not at his wages. Even Roger, who didn't have much pride left, recoiled at the thought of appearing in public in this getup. He was looking forward to seeing his manager's expression when he threw the costume in his face and walked out the door.

As a final touch, he cut the shape of a cloud out of a white hand towel and stitched it on carefully, using blue thread, as a central element for the front of the suit.

And then it was done.

It had taken him three days to finish the costume. To his surprise, he felt a twinge of pride in his handiwork. He held the suit up and examined it closely. It was perfect.

He was struck by a curious notion—what would be the harm in trying it on? Just for kicks, of course. It was not lost on him that the completion of his task marked the end of his gainful employment. Sadly, his job search for the past few days had not gone well. Prospective employers had taken one look at him and decided he was not their man. They were not impressed by his fresh haircut and carefully pressed shirt, and had pegged him right away as a harmless goofball. Likeable enough, but not the type of person who you would think of trusting with the keys to the store. It was the story of his life.

His mother would not be pleased to find him unemployed—again.

Stepping into the restroom, Roger stripped down to his skivvies and squeezed himself into the stretchy lycra suit. He pulled the hood section on over his head, leaving only the circle of his face and his hands bare, and took stock of

the results in the mirror. Hmm. He pretended he was holding his sale sign and struck a pose.

"Our mattresses will put you on cloud nine!" he declared
loudly.

Roger was a biggish man, and like many men his age,
he had picked up some belly fat over the years. He had the
kind of stomach shape that was associated with a fondness for
beer, which was true enough in his case. As it turned out, this
rotund body form was exactly what was needed to properly
fill out his cloud costume. Admiring himself in the mirror,
Roger was sure that some skinny college student, desperate
for cash, would not do the suit justice. It was a question of
bulk, and Roger had just the right amount of bulk in just the
right places.

He stared back at his own reflection. Wouldn't it be a hoot
to just go outside and try it out for a few minutes? He'd be able
to tell his boss that he'd given it a real shot. He knew he looked
ridiculous. But with most of his head covered by the suit, he
actually had a fair amount of anonymity. And at least he could
finally be sure, beyond a shadow of a doubt, that he'd hit rock
bottom. That, in its own way, was great news.

Here goes nothing, he said to himself, grabbing his sign
and stepping out into the store proper.

"I'm all done, boss!" he exclaimed.

His boss whirled around and inspected Roger's handiwork critically. "Not bad," he admitted grudgingly. "You took
your sweet time about it, don't think I don't know that. Now
get out there and let's sell some mattresses!" His boss put two
hands in the small of his back and pushed Roger toward the
exit. "Go get 'em, cloud man!"

Cloud Man? Roger wasn't sure how this moniker had escaped him. It was perfect. It had a certain superhero quality to it. His superpowers would be floating and putting villains to sleep.

Roger, aka Cloud Man, walked out of the store with a big grin on his face. Union Square South was a busy block, full of mostly young people bustling about. A number of local characters were scattered around selling trinkets off folding tables, or handing out flyers, but Roger immediately became the focus of everyone's attention. Heads swiveled. A young guy walking past gave him a high five.

"Hey marshmallow dude! Love the costume!"

"Actually, it's Cloud Man," Roger corrected him.

"Clouds? Marshmallows? Whatever, dude! Just do your thing."

"Yes, sir! I'm here to keep the city safe and make sure villains get a good night's sleep—with the fishes!"

This turned out to be the first of a large number of high fives, fist bumps, and even a few hugs. Roger's popularity soared through the roof. He was not used to this kind of attention, but it was strangely exhilarating. He had conversations with strangers, he danced around, he made funny faces. Wearing the costume made anything he'd ever wished he could do in public somehow possible.

Two hours later, an exhausted Roger took a break and went back inside, all thoughts of quitting his job anytime soon erased from his mind. He hadn't had this much fun in years.

Roger found his boss beaming. "Foot traffic is through the roof," he whispered to him, giving him a big thumbs-up. "I've sold six California Kings already today."

"No problem, boss, just putting in a good day's work. Now about that raise . . ."

His boss chuckled and clapped him on the shoulder. "Good one! Take your lunch break and be back outside in forty-five minutes."

Not bothering to change out of his costume, Roger hustled over to the diminutive falafel shop on 17th Street, snagged himself a hot sandwich, and walked into the park in search of a spot to sit and eat. His popularity had continued unabated. People took one look at him and assumed he was a barrel-of-laughs, kind of guy. Even the normally humorless falafel store guy had beamed and given him a free soda.

Union Square was crowded with people enjoying the intermittent sunshine, and the rows of benches in the interior of the park were packed. Roger cruised up and down the pathways until he finally saw an open spot up ahead. As he drew nearer he was taken aback by the sight of the bench's other occupant. A woman dressed in a pink bunny costume was sitting there eating a pretzel. Clearly the space was only open because other people were reluctant to sit next to her. How weird would it be if he, also dressed in a costume, sat down next to her? But it was a late lunch for him, and he was eager to tuck into his sandwich. Besides—he was on the clock.

He sat down hesitantly, stealing a sideways glance at the bunny woman as he unwrapped his sandwich. He took a little nibble, careful not to let tahini sauce drip on his costume.

"So who are you supposed to be?" The woman in the bunny suit was looking at him inquiringly.

Roger turned and smiled. "I'm Cloud Man! Making your sweet dreams a reality!"

"Cloud Man. That's adorable. Is your costume homemade?"

"Yes, I made it myself. Just finished it this morning."

"Well it's nice to meet you, Cloud Man. I'm Constance the Bunny."

"Glad to meet you, too, Constance the Bunny. Funny, the two of us both sitting here in costumes. Not even Halloween yet or anything."

"Yes, it's absurd. But, surprisingly, it's not the strangest thing to happen to me today."

"Seriously? So what was stranger than this then? If you don't mind me asking."

"Not at all. It so happens I saw an alien abduction up on a rooftop earlier."

"What did this alien look like?"

"It was big and round, with four skinny green arms and four big yellow eyes on its two heads. It grabbed some poor woman off a ladder. You won't be seeing her again anytime soon."

"Wow. That must have been quite a sight."

"Sure was. Threw me for a loop. Do you believe in aliens?"

Roger pondered her question for a moment. His bench-mate was obviously loony tunes. She seemed friendly and harmless, but definitely deranged. On the other hand—she was a real live woman, engaging him in friendly conversation. He couldn't remember the last time that had happened. And here he was sitting in a public park wearing a blue leotard covered in cotton balls. He was in no position to be slapping the crazy label on anyone.

Navigating the ins and outs of the dating scene for the past few years had been a bit of a nightmare for Roger. Most women's eyes would gloss over as soon as they discovered he was broke and living at home.

Roger swallowed the large bite he'd taken. "Well, I certainly don't rule out the possibility of aliens visiting our planet," he replied. There, that was a nice uncontroversial position to hold on the question of extraterrestrials. But feeling that perhaps this response might be seen as lukewarm by someone who claimed to have seen an extraterrestrial with her own two eyes earlier in the day, he decided to add a more ringing endorsement. "Come to think of it, when you do the math, you know—that whole number of galaxies multiplied by the number of planets thing—it seems downright inevitable."

"Yes, my thoughts exactly. Statistically probable. But quite different from actually seeing one yourself, of course."

"I can only imagine," Roger took another big bite out of his sandwich and munched it thoughtfully.

Passersby were stopping to take photos of them on the bench. Constance didn't seem bothered by this, so Roger decided he would ignore them too. Their conversation soon drifted to more ordinary topics, and Roger was surprised to discover that she worked as a stenographer. He had never met a stenographer before, but he had never pictured them to be the sort of people who walked around in pink bunny costumes.

Roger chose to be upfront and breezy about his own job and living situations. He found it much easier to be open and unembarrassed while dressed as Cloud Man. Expectations for a grown man wearing a wacky costume were clearly not that high. And if bunny girl made any snap judgments about him, she didn't show it.

"Must be a bit warm under there," Roger ventured, glancing at her fuzzy costume.

"No, I'm quite comfortable," she said. Leaning into him, she whispered, "I'm not wearing anything underneath. Don't tell anyone."

Roger felt his face grow warm. "Oh, I see. That will be our little secret then."

"How about you?"

"I decided to stick with my tidy whities."

"I suppose public decorum demands as much."

"Precisely."

Constance had finished her pretzel, and Roger could tell by the way she was looking around that she was getting restless.

"Well, Cloud Man, it's been nice chatting with you, but I think I'd better be heading home. I feel a nap coming on. It's my day off, you know."

"Oh. Enjoy your siesta then." He was disappointed she was leaving. There was something quite fascinating about her. The more he thought about it, the less the whole insanity thing bothered him. Why should crazy be a dealbreaker? Every woman he'd ever dated had a screw or two loose. At least bunny woman wasn't pretending to be anything she wasn't.

Constance stood up and stretched. Roger couldn't help noticing she had a nice figure. "Er, Constance, I don't suppose you'd be interested in meeting me for a drink later?"

He spit the words out before he had a chance to second-guess himself, racking his brain for the last time he had asked a stranger out. Yep, he'd definitely never done that before.

Must be the suit, he thought to himself. He smiled up at her nervously.

Constance cocked her head to one side, causing her bunny ears to flip in that direction. "I would like that," she replied, smiling. "Fair warning, though, you may have some catching up to do."

"Don't worry. I'll do my best to get up to speed. Do you have a favorite bar?"

"Do you know Ground Zero over on Second Ave?"

"Sure," he replied, "the one with the cheap pitchers of beer and the sawdust on the floor. I love that place."

"Great!" Shall we say seven o'clock?"

"Perfect. I'll be there at seven. Er . . . should we wear our costumes or civilian clothes?"

"Well, speaking for myself, it's a bunny costume kind of day."

"I see. Got a good thing going, so why stop now, I hear that. Costumes it is then."

"Fantastic," she said. "Hey, can I ask you—do you like rabbits?"

"Rabbits?"

"Yes. Rabbits. Real ones, I mean."

"It so happens I had a pet rabbit as a kid growing up. They are very underrated pets, if you ask me."

"Exactly, very underrated! Who needs a cat or a dog if they can have a rabbit?"

"So true."

Roger was astonished when she leaned in and gave him a peck on the cheek. "Thought I'd just test the waters," she explained with a giggle. Her breath smelled of mustard and tequila, and Roger found it intoxicating.

"You should probably tell me your real name," said Constance.

"Oh, it's Roger."

"Well, I'll see you later, Roger." She blew him another kiss and skipped away.

"See you at seven, Constance!"

Roger ate the last crumbs of his pita in a daze. He couldn't believe it. Rock bottom was so much better than he could have ever imagined. He wondered why it got such a bad rap.

20. OLLIE

[4 p.m.]

A gusty wind had picked up, whisking thick clouds across the sky, and prodding Ollie to zip his leather jacket. He'd spent the past hour trapped in one of the seven circles of Hell—trudging miserably around the East Village, taping missing cat posters to lampposts, each one an unwelcome reminder. Okay, so maybe it wasn't on the official list of Hell's circles, but if they were ever looking to expand to say ten, Ollie was sure it would make the cut. He kept getting pitying glances from strangers when they stopped to read the poster, and he wasn't sure how many more of them he could take.

And if Pirate had been zapped by that bizarre creature, then all his hard work would be for nothing.

He made a right on Sixth Street, heading west, and his eyes locked on a familiar banner fluttering up ahead. The

Empress Café was a popular neighborhood hangout. The owner, Miss Ruby, had hit on the idea of combining a restaurant with a psychic parlor so she could showcase both her family recipes and her talents as a prognosticator. She'd hung vintage tarot posters throughout, giving the place a trippy vibe that had made it a hit with the locals. Ollie, who liked to stop in for their hot chocolate, was a familiar face in the Café. Miss Ruby was always friendly and chatty toward him, and never minded if he sat on a stool for an hour sipping his drink and reading the store paper.

He pressed his face up to the window and spotted Miss Ruby behind the counter—she was in her mid-thirties, with an ample figure, warm skin, and bushy hair. Ollie pushed through the double doors. "Hello, Miss Ruby," Ollie said gloomily, pulling a flyer from the messenger bag slung over his shoulder and handing it to her. "Do you mind if I pin this up on your board?"

"Oh no! Ollie!" she said when she caught sight of the "Lost Cat" headline. "This is terrible news." She grilled him about the details of Pirate's disappearance and seemed genuinely pained to hear them. "It's not the best missing cat photo I've ever seen," she pointed out, squinting at the picture and turning the paper sideways to try and make sense of it.

"I found out the hard way," Ollie explained, "that a checkered cat plus a patchwork bedspread, run through a copier, equals inkblot."

"That's quite a generous reward you've got tacked on there," a long purple nail pointed to the 150 dollar figure he had triple underlined in the poster.

"I figured it couldn't hurt."

"Except your bank account maybe."

"Yeah, except for that," he admitted.

"I didn't know you had that kind of money."

"I don't. I mean—paying the reward will clean me out." Not to mention he'd just been fired from his job.

"You sure do love your kitty." She handed him back the flyer and waved him toward the bulletin board. "Go right ahead, you never know who might see it."

Ollie wandered over to the board and stuck two silver thumbtacks into the top corners of his flyer. When he returned to the counter, Miss Ruby had a mug of hot chocolate ready for him, and she surprised him by waving away his attempt to pay for it. Then she offered to give him a tarot card reading on the house.

"If you are going through a personal crisis, you would be wise to check the cards. Then at least you'll know what you are up against."

Ollie wasn't sure if he believed in the cards. But he'd always been curious about them and didn't see how he could say no to a free reading. Grabbing his mug, he followed her through heavy velvet curtains into the back room, where he sat down opposite her at a long mahogany table. She turned on a stained glass table lamp and began to shuffle a deck of ornate tarot cards.

"I want you to focus on your question," she said, her voice suddenly dramatic. "Turn your question over in your mind, and then pick three cards." In a practiced motion, she spread the cards out in a line on the table and watched him intently.

Ollie took a sip of the creamy chocolaty liquid. One question had been floating front and center in his mind all day—did I really see an alien? But he wasn't planning on telling another soul about that. Instead he informed Miss Ruby that his question was "where is Pirate?" He pulled three cards from different spots and handed them to her without looking at them. She set them facedown in a row that started on his left and then turned the first one over with a flourish.

It was the Hanged Man, and showed a man hanging by his ankle from a post. Ollie grimaced—not a good start. Gesturing to the card, Miss Ruby said, "The Hanged Man signifies being suspended in time. This card represents Pirate, who at the moment is trapped in a state of uncertainty. We don't know where he is, or how he is doing, and until we find out, you are both stuck in a limbo of sorts."

Uncertainty? That was exactly the feeling that had been gnawing at him all day. This card was right on the money. He eyed the next card nervously as she flipped it over—the Devil. Ollie sucked in his breath. There it was, a drawing of a horned and winged satan, sitting on a throne. Judging from her expression, Miss Ruby was a bit shocked, and her hands hovered above the card as if it were giving off heat.

"In the middle spot, we find old Baphomet himself," she said, her voice now theatrically low. "I wish I could put a kind interpretation on this, but to me, this card, following on the heels of the last one, says that your circumstances were not caused purely by chance. There is a force of darkness some-where conspiring against you."

"Yeah, actually, I'm not surprised to hear that." Ollie did

his best to feign nonchalance, but in his mind, he was sure the Devil must correspond to the creature he'd seen this morning.

"Is there something you are not telling me?" she skewered him with a penetrating stare.

"Er. No. I just mean that it seems like the whole world is set against me today."

"Well don't give up hope. The last card is often the most telling as to the resolution." Ollie suspected the last card would be ominous too. She turned it over and he was surprised to see that it was the Star, with an innocuous drawing of a nude woman dipping a jar into a lake.

"Now, this last card is much more promising," she said. "The Star tells us that a higher consciousness is also in play behind the scenes. It is an auspicious card. It suggests you should have faith, and be open to help from unexpected sources."

"What does that mean exactly?"

"This card is balancing out the middle card. There is a tension there. Things could go either way, but make sure you welcome any help you can get. All three cards are from the major Arcana, so I suspect there is more at stake in the outcome of your search than you may realize." She extended her arms, palms out in a that's-it gesture.

"Thanks, Miss Ruby. I guess I'd better get back to posting flyers." He gulped down what was left of his hot chocolate while she scooped up the cards and slipped them back into their box.

21. ZARA

[6 p.m.]

Zara stood face-to-face with the security guard, separated from him by a glass door. She had arrived just as he was locking up, and her urgent pleading had fallen on deaf ears. He was unmoved when she pointed to the sign that said the shelter closed at six and then at her watch, which showed there were seven minutes left until the top of the hour. Accurate timekeeping was clearly not on his list of things to worry about in life.

She politely explained once more that she just needed to take a quick look for a lost cat, trying to appeal to his better nature. But he didn't seem to have one. He just gave her a callous shrug. Evidently lost cats did not rank very high on his list either.

Zara was distressed. She didn't want to have to tell Ollie she had arrived at the shelter right after it closed. She'd wanted to do this for him as a peace gesture, to show that she was sorry for biting his head off earlier. He was having a rough time, and she knew he needed her help, even if he insisted on being a stubborn fool.

Zara studied the heavyset man on the other side of the glass. His gray uniform was at least one size too small for him, and the crooked name tag on his shirt identified him as Hugo. He looked like a Hugo—he had a thin mustache, a few inexplicable wisps of hair on his chin, and short-cropped black hair. He was built along the lines of a small shed, and she guessed that blocking people's way was probably something that came naturally to him. He had clearly gone into the right line of work.

There was a smug expression on his face that he was making no effort to hide. Zara decided to approach the situation logically. She made a mental list of the advantages the security guard had over her. For one, he had the keys to the locked door. For another, his hefty size guaranteed him the advantage in a physical confrontation. And that was about it. In her own favor, she put down better dressed, which was true even though she was wearing a ratty old sweater. She added better personal hygiene below that and was momentarily grateful there was a barrier between them. And last but not least she stuck higher IQ in her own column.

It occurred to her that of the three, it was this last one that held out the most hope for getting her past this human roadblock. So Zara furrowed her brow as she racked her brain for a way to wipe that smug expression off his face.

Moments later she had a glimmer of an idea. Yes, that just might work. She gave Hugo a broad smile as she reached into her wallet and extracted a ten-dollar bill. She held it up and gave it a crisp little snap for him to see, then she squatted down and slipped it smoothly under the door. She stood up and cocked her head at him.

"Ball's in your court," she said cheerily.

As she saw it, Hugo had two options. He could treat her ten dollars as a bribe and let her in, which he wasn't likely to do, considering that the camera in the lobby entrance was trained on the door. He wouldn't want to put his job at risk for a measly ten bucks. His second option was to take the high road and return the money to her, possibly throwing in a stern speech about his high ethical standards.

As she predicted, he settled for option two. Grimacing and shooting her an indignant look, he bent down, picked up her money, reached for a set of keys hooked on his belt, and unlocked the door. He cracked the door open, stuffed a beefy arm through, and handed the money back to her. "Listen, miss, I don't know what you are trying to pull, but that sort of thing isn't going to work on me."

"I'm sorry, Mr. Hugo. I was feeling desperate." Zara took back the ten-dollar bill and shoved it in her purse. "Now, how about you let me through seeing as how it isn't actually closing time yet?"

"By my watch, it is. And once the door is locked, it stays locked. That's my rule."

"I see." Zara smiled impudently. She was tempted to point out that the door was in fact unlocked, but was worried his tiny brain might blow a fuse.

In the meantime Hugo pushed the door closed again. That is to say he tried to. Unfortunately for him her foot was jammed in the doorframe, preventing him from closing it again.

Fury registered in his eyes. "Miss, I'm going to ask you just once to move your foot."

"Or what? Are you going to slam the door shut and break my toes? Are you going to come out here and arrest me? Is that the sort of incident you want to deal with at this late hour in the day? Think of how long you will be here filling out paperwork, waiting for the police to ask all their questions. Heck, think about the potential lawsuit. If I were you, I would be very careful about what you do next, because your cushy little job may be at stake."

Hugo's first approach was to try and nudge her foot out of the way with his own black-booted foot, but that proved ineffective. She had wedged her foot in there good and proper. Watching his eyes, she could see his mental wheels grinding away slowly as her words began to sink in. It seemed to take a herculean effort for him to control his temper. They remained locked in a standoff for a long moment. But, unable to close the door or get her to move her foot away, he finally just threw the door open and shot her a look that could have curdled milk.

"There, are you happy?" he growled. "You're lucky you caught me in a good mood today. We close in three minutes! You'd better do whatever you came here to do super fast or I will personally escort you off the premises."

"Thank you, Hugo, you're a real gem." Zara hit him with a smug little smile of her own as she scooted past him and hurried toward the reception area.

The front desk was manned by a subdued woman in a

blue lab coat who seemed vaguely perplexed to see someone coming in at that hour. Zara guessed she was probably some sort of volunteer, and she hastily asked her if it was possible to take a quick look for a missing cat. The woman had kind eyes, with a fringe of black hair falling over a moon-shaped face.

"He's my friend's cat, actually. He's out posting flyers, and I told him I would check the closest shelter. He's called Pirate. The cat, I mean, not my friend."

"I see. Well it looks like you are the last visitor for the day, so let's go see if Pirate has turned up here, shall we? Are you sure you will recognize your friend's cat? I don't have to tell you how many cats are carbon copies of each other."

"Yes, don't worry. Pirate is very distinctive. He's a large black and white cat with yellow eyes. And he has a black patch over one eye."

"Is he chipped?"

"No, I'm afraid not."

"Does he have a tag?"

"No collar, no tag either."

"I see. We get that a lot around here. Do you have a photo?"

"No, not on me, I'm afraid. But my friend has some pictures of him. If we find him, I'm sure he can fax them over quickly if you need proof of ownership."

"That won't be necessary. We are just happy when any of our cats finds a home. Come to think of it, I remember a lady dropping off a black-and-white cat earlier today. A real bruiser she found in her yard. Let's go take a look and see if we can arrange a happy reunion."

Hearing this, Zara's pulse quickened. She let herself be

led down dimmed hallways, up a staircase, and through a series of doors. The old prewar building was a windowless maze. She didn't want to get her hopes up, but the cat this woman had described certainly sounded a heck of a lot like Pirate. She let herself imagine how grateful Ollie would be if she returned with Pirate in her arms.

The woman led Zara through several musty rooms filled with walls of caged cats, who greeted them with loud mewing. Zara peered into each crate. Seeing animals cooped up like this always got to her. Sometimes it seemed to her that there were an infinite amount of small tragedies in the world.

When they reached the last roomful of cats, her guide walked straight over to a crate at the far end and scrutinized its occupant. She glanced back at her clipboard and then gestured toward the cage interior with her ballpoint pen. "Is that him?" she asked. "This is the cat that matches your description. He just joined us this afternoon."

Zara rushed over and peered intently into the crate's dim interior. A huge, shaggy black-and-white cat was curled up inside. Her heart leapt. Then the animal turned to look at her with scared blue eyes, and her hopes were dashed.

22. MANOLO

[6 p.m.]

Manolo had spent the last hour installing a dishwasher. It had taken much longer than expected, and the tenant had been standing over him the whole time. But hopefully it was his last big job for the day. He returned home to his ground floor apartment and was surprised to discover the aroma of lamb chops was in the air. The dish was a childhood favorite of his, but Natalya had only ever made it once, right before they became engaged. For the next three years, she had waved off his requests, saying that it was an expensive meal and a lot of trouble to cook until he'd eventually stopped asking for it.

"How was your day, my darling?" asked Natalya.

"What? Oh, you talkin' to me? No complaints, I guess. Um . . . are you feeling okay?"

"Yes, my darling, I feel great. I remembered how much

you used to love rosemary lamb chops with papas fritas, and it's been so long that I decided to make them for you."

"Great . . . er . . . thanks?" Manolo was feeling very confused.

"Let me bring you a beer. You sit down and put your feet up, I'm sure you must have had a long day."

Moving slowly, Manolo did as instructed, sliding into the armchair she was leading him to. Cautiously he put his feet up on the edge of the tattered ottoman. Sitting there was a strange feeling, as this chair was typically reserved for Natalya's exclusive use. Normally he didn't dare sit here, even when she wasn't home. But there was something very strange in the air. He took a cautious sip from the frosty bottle she handed him. It tasted normal. He nearly jumped out of his skin when she leaned down and gave him a peck on the cheek. Manolo's eyebrows shot up.

His mind raced a mile a minute trying to find some explanation for the unrecognizable home scene he had stumbled into. He looked around at the furniture and the walls to make sure he hadn't mistakenly walked into the wrong apartment. But there was the framed photograph of Aunt Rita on the mantelpiece, and one of their cats lay sprawled on the radiator case, staring back at him as if it also sensed something was amiss. He tried to remember the last time Natalya had kissed him. He had nearly given up hope for seeing any affection from her, in much the same way he had become resigned to never tasting Aunt Rita's lamb chops again.

A smiling Natalya brought over a small bowl filled with stuffed green olives. As she bent down to place it on the coffee table, Manolo noticed a tan bandage on her shoulder.

"What happened to your arm, Natalya?" he asked.

"Oh, this? It's nothing, just a scratch. I don't even remember how I got it!"

"You don't remember?"

"Nope. But don't worry, I'm feeling great. You're the one I'm worried about, my darling. You work too hard." She scuttled back to her sizzling stove.

Manolo leaned back into the chair, deep in thought. The way he saw it, there were two possible explanations for Natalya's odd behavior. One was that she had somehow found out about his little adventure, and maybe even about the money stash in the basement, and she was setting him up. If that was the case, she would let him have it in a big way the moment he dropped his guard, quite possibly with the very same knife she was now using to crush the garlic. The second, more appealing possibility, was that she'd hit her head, or had some sort of mini stroke. That would also explain her odd memory lapse.

Either way he decided it would be best to just sit tight, ride it out, and do his best to enjoy the lamb chops, which smelled amazing. Even if he did feel like a death row inmate being served his last meal. Manolo assumed the blank expression of someone who was completely resigned to their fate. He sat there in Natalya's special chair, sweating profusely, silently sipping his beer, and waiting for the blow to fall. It was at that moment that a third option occurred to him. Could it be possible that his offering—his stupid Santa Muerte candle, the cheap necklace he had draped on the statue . . . no, it was too fantastic, it just couldn't be. The odds that he was losing his mind were higher than that.

This new fourth option struck him as full of real possibility, and in his head he ticked off a list of all the strange behaviors he'd taken part in lately. Yes, if he was a gambling man he would put his money on option four. The attendants from Bellevue were probably on their way over right now, bringing a straightjacket with his name on it. Natalya was just keeping him distracted until they arrived to cart him away. Yep, that must be it for sure.

23. AXZLEPROVA

[6:45 p.m.]

AxzleProva went through their preflight checklist once more. Both of their expressions were brooding, and they were silent except for any required flight related communications. After the unfortunate second incident this afternoon, it had become clear to them that the whole mission had to be scrapped. A human had actually scaled the side of their ship, and there was no way to downplay the seriousness of their situation.

Protocol was strict on what to do if their cover was blown—first they were to do their best to mitigate the situation, and then they were to depart as soon as a stealthy takeoff became possible.

The bio-reprogramming of the intruder had gone better than expected. They had successfully erased her memory of them, and they had taken advantage of the opportunity to perform some minor cognitive adjustments, lowering her overactive contempt pathways and boosting her very weak capacity for remorse. In spite of her clear mental fortitude, the psychological tweaks had quickly taken hold. These small changes no doubt amounted to significant improvements on her original mindset, and would likely improve her overall happiness levels considerably. Still, HQ would not be mollified by this. A failed mission would go on their permanent record. And while this was something that happened to all field agents occasionally, they would have to be even more careful going forward, because if they racked up too many botched missions, they would be suspended from duty. Remaining unnoticed was the first and most important rule for covert observation postings.

Not interfering in local matters was rule two, and clearly by resetting the intruder's brain patterns, they had also broken this rule. They would be obligated to include it in their report. That they suspected the woman's new outlook on life would be a big improvement was of little consequence as far as HQ was concerned.

The likelihood that this intruder or anyone else would be back to investigate the roof was pretty slim, but it was not a chance they were permitted to take. All their promising research had come to a grinding halt, and they would have to go back to base for a refit since their vessel had been designed with this specific spot in mind. There they would have to wait for a new location to be selected and a new ship to be drawn up and built, procedures that could drag on interminably. The likelihood that they would be chosen to return to planet

Earth was pretty slim, a fact that saddened them both, as they had warmed to this posting.

AxzleProva were not just dejected. They were also furious with humans, a species that they had very little patience for. These humans were meddling and murderous overgrown monkeys, and the whole planet was infested with them. For now at least, they were confined to this small backwater world, but they shuddered to think of what would happen if humans ever found their way out into the greater galaxy or beyond.

With all the preparations complete, there was nothing left for them to do but sit and wait. Once the cover of darkness settled over the city, they would trigger a power outage in the vicinity, activate their signal scramblers, and lift off.

24. MRS. BUTLER

[6:45 p.m.]

Mrs. Butler stared into the cage. The monstrous cat locked eyes with her, unblinking. She had to concede he was a worthy opponent. She knew he must be very hungry by now, but he hadn't touched the food laced with rat poison that she had slipped him through the bars of the cage. It would seem she had a picky eater on her hands.

He was noisy, too, and had meowed loudly for hours in a demanding tone. She'd thrown a heavy blanket over the cage, but five minutes later he'd managed to pull it off with his claws. This impasse was driving her over the edge. She felt trapped herself, with no good way out, and she wasn't sure how she would make it through the night again with this god-awful creature sitting in her dining room.

At that moment Colonel Blake materialized in her kitchen right before her eyes, paler and more transparent than his photograph, but with the same haughty bearing and blazing eyes.

"Nora, you yellow-bellied coward," he bellowed. "Just slit that foul creature's throat and throw his guts out for the buzzards to feed on!"

Taken aback, Mrs. Butler pleaded with her ancestor.

"I can't! It's too much! I'm just going to have to let him go. He has me beat!"

"Surrender? A Butler never surrenders! Fight to the death! Yours or his. Tooth and claw. Victory or death!" With this last outburst, her forbearer drew his ghostly sword and charged out into the living room, where he quickly dissipated into nothingness.

This brief exchange with her ancestor left Mrs. Butler feeling ashamed. Colonel Blake was right. Intestinal fortitude was the answer. She needed to dig deep and steel her resolve. She dismissed from her mind the option of releasing the feline since she refused to dishonor her family by losing a battle of wills with a cat. Instead she began to prepare herself mentally for the task of dispatching the beast. She examined the knives in her butcher block and settled on a long and skinny kitchen knife as the best choice for reaching him through the cage bars.

If she was going to do this, then it was better to get it over and done with. There was no time like the present.

She turned to face the cage, knife in hand. Just then— the phone rang. She did her best to ignore it, but perhaps because of her many years as a secretary, ignoring phones was impossible for her. So she set the knife down on the counter.

"I doubt it's the governor calling to grant you a reprieve," she hissed at the cat, who was watching her intently. Cackling at her own joke, she picked up the receiver.

It turned out to be one of her nephews. He was calling her because he had some clients in town who he had promised to take out to dinner. He needed his favorite aunt to step in and watch over her seven-year-old goddaughter for a few hours. She did her best to politely decline, saying she wasn't feeling well. But apparently his phone call was a mere formality, as he was already in the car on his way over to drop the child off. Her nephew even had the gall to suggest that he was being helpful by delivering his daughter to her door. Mrs. Butler wished she could just refuse outright—perhaps she should tell him that she had her hands full at the moment slaughtering a giant cat. That would make him think twice about using her as a free babysitting service. But instead she just bit her tongue and grudgingly consented. The damn cat would get a reprieve after all. It would be a few hours before she could carry out the grisly task. Then she would bury him in the yard in the dead of night. And maybe that would serve as a warning to any other cats in the neighborhood.

She agreed to meet her nephew out front at seven o'clock on the nose, which was just a few minutes away. The lack of advance notice rankled her. With trepidation and great effort, she grabbed the cage handle, dragged it over to the coat closet, and kicked it inside, ignoring the hisses and growls let out by the angry brute. Then she tuned the radio on the console table to the local classical music station and turned the volume up high on a soothing Schubert sonata in B-flat.

25. CASSANDRA

[7 p.m.]

S he got off the subway at Astor Place and walked east. The sidewalks were crowded with people heading home from work, people with steady jobs and regular paychecks. And what was *she* busy doing? Traipsing around the city to unpaid auditions that never panned out. Cassandra felt the familiar prickle of doubt about her life choices.

Today's callback had been a surreal experience. In the small waiting room, she had shared a bench with two other hopefuls, girls who looked exactly like her. It was like looking in a mirror, or two mirrors to be exact. The three of them sat there quietly for hours as delay followed delay until finally, one of the two dead ringers had been called in. The other girl had gone next, leaving Cassandra sitting alone on the bench, listening through the wall to the scene being run over and over, until it was finally her turn. Then she'd gone through the same motions as the other two girls—knocking repeatedly on a door and seductively delivering her big line: "Your Pop-Tarts are ready," to the middle-aged stand-in for a pajama-clad teenage boy. Hold up the product, big smile. The director, a man with a booming voice and slicked-back hair, had demanded that she show "more pizzazz", and yelled at her to "make it pop," just as he had with her doppelgängers before her.

On days like today, Cassandra felt so inconsequential. She knew that only a lucky few would make it big, and for everybody else it was just years of rejection before being forced to quit, and then . . . what? A career as a professional waitress? She shuddered at the thought.

Things would've been so much easier if only Jeremy, her college boyfriend, had moved here with her, like they had planned. He was an art installer and could easily have found work in New York, but he'd gotten cold feet at the last minute and accepted a job in San Francisco instead. They had called it quits, and she had taken the plunge all by her lonesome. She'd heard through mutual friends that Jeremy was already seeing someone new—that schmuck. He knew how much moving to New York meant to her. This was the city where her mother had lived when she'd been about the age Cassandra was now, working as a dancer and living at the Barbizon on the Upper East Side. Being here made Cassandra feel like she was walking in her mother's footsteps.

Cassandra jogged across First Avenue just as the light was changing and scooted down Sixth Street. The Empress Café was on her way home, and she was counting on their corn chowder for an easy dinner. Served with a hunk of their flatbread, it was to die for. Although it was probably like a million calories. Cassandra smiled wryly—she had earned that soup today, sitting on that bench for hours.

Inside, the café was jammed with the usual dinner crush. The take-out line wasn't too bad, shorter at least than the other line in the back of people waiting to get their palms read. *That* was not something Cassandra ever intended to waste her money on. She only ever came here to grab take-away, or occasionally for their dark roast in the mornings.

When she reached the register, the girl took her order and scooped her soup hurriedly into a container from a large tureen behind the counter. Cassandra had to remind her about the bread. She couldn't wait to get home and dig in, but she still stopped on her way out to give the bulletin board a once-over. She liked to keep tabs on local events, and it was always possible someone interesting could be looking for a roommate. A pink lost cat flyer jumped out at her right away. She squinted at the hand-printed words—Large Black and White Cat, Male, Yellow Eyes—and then did her best to unscramble the cat shape in the blotchy photo. Once she did, it hit her—there could be no mistake. This was the big cat that crazy lady had trapped last night. Someone was trying to find him. There was a row of tabs along the bottom with the phone number for someone named Oliver. Cassandra quickly tore off a corner and tucked it into her wallet.

Back home, Cassandra kicked off her shoes and headed straight for the kitchen phone, extending the portable hand-set's telescopic antenna. She was nervous about calling up some stranger, but she took a deep breath and screwed up her resolve—she had to help that cat if she could. She punched the number into the touch-tone keypad, and the phone rang five times on the other end before an answering machine picked up.

"Hi, this is Ollie, you know what to do!"

Cassandra left a short message and her number and hung up. She began to eat her soup, with the phone ready close by, but it still hadn't rung by the time she was done with her meal. What she needed now, more than anything else in the world, was a nice hot bath, so she decided she would just put the handset on the sill of the tub. Answering a call in there might be a bit awkward, but so long as she avoided any splashing, she should be fine.

She dropped the plug in the tub, squirted in a generous amount of bubble bath, and opened up the tap. She pulled the drapes closed in the living room and turned on a pair of lamps, giving the room a warm glow. Then she disappeared into the bedroom, reemerging moments later in a white terry cloth robe.

Back in the bathroom, she hung the robe on the door. Stepping into the tub, she lowered herself slowly through a thick layer of creamy foam and leaned back with a contented sigh. She let herself daydream about what life would be like once she landed a juicy role on a television series. She imagined different people she knew seeing her on-screen for the first time. Would they pick up the phone and call her in amazement? Of course, they would have to go through her personal assistant first. And when Jeremy called her to tell her he had broken up with his new girlfriend, she would get on the line and say "Jeremy? Jeremy who?"

After a few minutes of soaking, Cassandra pinched off

her nose with her thumb and forefinger and let herself sink into the water, her eyes squeezed tightly shut. She held her breath for a minute, lying still in the echoey blackness. Resurfacing, she swept bubbles and glistening strands of dark hair from her face.

The phone rang about fifteen minutes into her bath, just as she'd finished shaving her legs. She sat up, dabbed her hands on a towel, and stared at the ringing handset. It might be her dad calling again, or it could be that Oliver guy calling her back. There was only one way to find out.

She pushed the button. "Hello?"

"Hello? Is this Cassandra? My name is Oliver. You called me about my missing cat?"

26. OLLIE

[7 p.m.]

Done posting flyers, Ollie made his way home down a darkened Fourth Street. The headlamps of passing cars sent shadows streaking across the narrow sidewalk. When he arrived at his building, he found Zara sitting on the terra cotta steps waiting for him. He was flooded with a sense of relief. She hadn't given up on him after all.

She jumped to her feet as he approached and surprised him by throwing her arms around him and hugging him tightly. Ollie held her close, his face pressed into her hair, wondering if there was a button somewhere he could press that would freeze time.

She whispered that she was sorry about before, while he insisted to her that it had all been his own fault. She told him that she hadn't had any luck at the shelter and he thanked her for trying. It had been a long shot, anyway. They headed inside and started up the stairs toward the top floor.

The only indication of life in the quiet building was the sound of a blaring television somewhere. Crooked brass sconces gave off a shallow light which fell unevenly on stained and peeling wallpaper. Their footsteps made no sound on the frayed carpeting as Ollie trudged upward, leading the way, his hand gliding along the wooden banister.

Turning a bend in the stairs, a figure in a fuzzy pink outfit clattered into him. It was a woman dressed, rather bizarrely, in a bunny costume. He only realized it was Constance when she snarled at him and demanded that he watch where he was going. He apologized, and she sniffed disdainfully, but her demeanor softened slightly when she caught sight of Zara.

"You're not planning on going up to the roof are you?" Constance asked sharply.

"Er. I don't think so," he replied.

"I would steer clear if I were you. I was up there earlier and I witnessed an alien abduction."

Ollie's eyes grew wide and he gave Zara a what-do-you-think-of-that look. "What do you mean, exactly?" Ollie asked his fleece-clad neighbor curiously.

"Oh, you wouldn't believe me if I told you. And I'm afraid I don't have time to chat. I'm late for a date."

"Was it a giant green turtle with two heads?" Ollie asked quickly before she could push past him. She looked at him, startled.

"How would you know that?" she demanded, mystified.

"Are people in the building already gossiping about me? Saying I'm off my rocker? I guess the news of my mental breakdown is spreading fast." Her breath reeked of alcohol. He opened his mouth to tell her that he had also seen the creature, but she brushed past him quickly and disappeared down the stairs, her floppy pink ears bobbing out of sight as she turned the corner.

"Who was that?" whispered Zara.

"Constance. My downstairs neighbor."

"The one who yells at you about the noise?"

"That would be her," Ollie said over his shoulder.

"I'd never pictured her being quite so pink and fluffy."

"Never mind her outfit. Did you hear what she said?"

"I sure did. But I'm not sure she's the best character witness, if that's what you're thinking."

"C'mon, Zara, we can't both have made up the same exact story."

"Unless you two are in cahoots," she said, grinning. "Or maybe it's something in the water?"

"You can't mean that," Ollie said huffily.

"Relax. Don't get your knickers in a twist," she said with a chuckle. "You're right. This totally backs you up. Although I still think someone is playing an elaborate prank on the neighborhood. But it's a relief to know you're not crazy. Not that I ever thought—"

"Yeah, not for a second, I'm sure," Ollie said with a smirk.

Upstairs his apartment was quiet, and there were no messages on the answering machine. Ollie grabbed two root beers from the fridge while Zara plucked a 10,000 Maniacs album from a crate of records on the floor and popped it onto his record player. She began to sway slowly to the music, and Ollie was suddenly very conscious of being alone with her in his small studio apartment. It wasn't her first visit, but on prior visits, Pirate had always been here to distract them.

Maybe she felt the same way, because after a few minutes she suggested they step out onto the fire escape, saying she'd love to catch a glimpse of the mysterious rooftop creature if he was out making the rounds.

"We'll see if you still think it's a fake when you see it with your own eyes," Ollie said. "Hopefully you won't be abducted. Or vaporized. I'd hate to be proven right that way."

"I'll take my chances." Zara grinned. "I just hope I have enough advance warning to activate my deflector shield. It takes a few seconds to warm up, you know."

"Hilarious."

He pushed up the window and they climbed out onto the fire escape. He pointed out the water tower, looming above them on their left, silhouetted against a gray illuminated sky. There was no sign of anything out of the ordinary. There were no giant two-headed space turtles, and, more disappointingly, no black-and-white cat anywhere to be seen. The courtyards below were an impenetrable mass of shadows.

Ollie settled down on the fire escape, his legs dangling in the well of the ladder and his gaze fixed on the nearby rooftop. Zara sat down beside him, leaning back against the building and hugging her knees. They sipped their root beers and listened to Natalie Merchant's voice through the open window. Lights were starting to go on in apartments across the way—the lives of strangers made suddenly transparent at the flick of a switch.

"It's too bad we had to cancel our jam session tonight," Zara said.

"Yeah, I'd been looking forward to it all week."

"Hey, don't you think it's high time we gave the band a name? Something fun? Then we could go around telling people we were in a rock band called the Spitting Cobras or something badass like that."

"That would be cool," Ollie said noncommittally.

"You don't sound terribly enthusiastic," Zara pointed out.

Ollie was silent for a long moment. "Have I ever told you I used to be in a band? Back in Indiana?"

"No. This is the first I've heard of it."

"It was a bit of a disaster. It was me and two of my high school friends—Joey and Leo. Our band was called Crocodile Smile."

"Good name."

"We had so much fun playing together in school that after graduation, we bought a used van, loaded up our gear, and hit the road. For the next six months, we managed to land sets at small venues, working for peanuts and the thrill of seeing our band name printed in the town weeklies."

"What happened? Did things just fizzle out?"

"Not exactly. One day I showed up to sound check at a bar in Milwaukee, and Joey and Leo—my two best friends in the whole world, mind you—sat me down and told me they had decided to bring another guitarist into the band. This guy we'd run into backstage a few times who had some modest recording success with a couple big names. They went on to say that since they didn't need two guitarists, I was out of the band."

"They didn't," Zara gasped.

"They did. And they kept all the songs I wrote too."

"Oh my god, that's just horrible. I'm really sorry that happened to you, Ollie. But . . . Miguel, Wally, and me—we would never do something like that. You know that, right?"

"I know. It's still hard to put it all on the line again."

"Well, newsflash, genius—the worst thing you could do is let those two jerks stop you from chasing your dream."

"Yeah, you're right."

"We've all had the rug pulled out from under us once or twice."

"Even you?"

"What do you mean *even me*?" she said indignantly. "Are you under the impression my life is a bed of roses? Because that is far from the case."

"How so? Enlighten me."

Zara took a deep breath and let it out. "I guess we're swapping hard-luck stories tonight. Okay, here we go. I don't think I ever told you about my ex-boyfriend, Richard." Ollie frowned and shook his head. He would have remembered that. "We dated for a couple years, but we broke up in April when I found out he'd been cheating on me every chance he got."

"So when you came to New York, you were fresh off a breakup? Why didn't you tell me about him?"

"I didn't want to come across all brokenhearted and pitiful."

"Fair enough. But you still should've mentioned it. Seems

like you might've used New York to put him in the rearview mirror?"

"Yeah, maybe. But his running around on me was just a part of it. The bigger problem was getting sucked into a circle of friends who were all wealthy trust fund types. All they ever talked about was shopping, going to the spa, getting wasted, and what exotic hot spot or ski resort they were jetting off to next. And when my relationship went up in smoke, they all pretended that I was making a big deal over nothing. Like it was me who was ruining everything by being stuffy, and it was all in my head."

"Unbelievable. Richard sounds like a real jackass if you ask me."

"He is. That is exactly what he is. Thank you, I've been searching for the right word to describe him for months, and you've just nailed it on the first go. He pretended to be this debonair man about town. But shave his head and take away his gold card, and you wouldn't have much left."

"Good hair then?"

"Yes. I can't deny it."

"I never realized your life over there was so swanky. Who knew you were such a fancy pants?"

"But I'm not. I'm not posh!" she protested. "I don't care about any of those things. All I've ever cared about is helping animals. And making music."

"Me, Miguel, and Wally must've made a pretty good snob recovery program."

"You were perfect. Just what the doctor ordered."

"But in a couple months you'll be headed back to your life there. What's your plan, vis-à-vis these blue-blooded jerks?"

"I'm going to throw out my address book and just start from scratch."

Ollie had no response to this. Starting from scratch would also mean putting her time in New York behind her. How long would it take her to forget all about him? Who knew if he would ever see her again? It's not like he could afford to fly to London and visit her. He was broke, out of a job, and would probably be forced to buy a one-way bus ticket home within a month.

"I can't believe you never told me about your life in London before."

"I didn't want you guys to peg me as some silver spoon rich kid."

"For the record, you've never struck me as being spoiled."

"Exactly. It worked! But—no more secrets. For either of us. Okay?" Then she leaned in and put her head on his shoulder and he put his arm around her. His heart and his mind were both racing: He felt like he was standing at the end of a cliff. That if he took another step, he would find himself plummeting into the abyss forever. As always, his thoughts went to her inevitable move back home in December. It was a roadblock they could never get past.

With a heavy sigh, she pulled away from him. "I'll be right back. I need to use the loo." He watched her duck back inside, and a minute later he heard the toilet flush. Then her voice rang out through the open window.

"Ollie?" she said. "Are you sure your telephone ringer is on?"

"What? Yes. I mean, I'm pretty sure. I do turn it off sometimes at night and forget to switch it back on."

"Well, here's the thing. There's a blinking red light on your answering machine that wasn't there before. Let me guess, you turned the volume off on that too?"

Ollie launched himself through the window onto his bed and scrambled to hit play on the message.

27. MRS. BUTLER

[7 p.m.]

Mrs. Butler stood in her kitchen, slowly honing her kitchen knife on a steel sharpening rod. She slid the long knife back and forth along the rod in a slow, methodical motion. Her eyes were bloodshot, and her face was set in a grim smile. In the nearby living room, the high pitched squeaks of cartoon voices emanated from the television. Sitting cross-legged in front of it, staring unblinkingly at the screen, was young Julia, her blond hair pushed back in a headband.

Nora Butler was thankful that so far the creature from hell had kept quiet in the closet. She wondered if he had finally gone to sleep in the dark, and wished she'd had the sense to chuck the cage in there a lot earlier. In the meantime she'd mentally committed to a course of action that would rid her of the cat for good, so she could get some sleep tonight.

She would follow her initial instincts and stab the critter as many times as necessary. But, critically, it had occurred to her that she needed a plastic tarp to put under the cage to catch any blood and guts that splattered around the scene.

She was no longer worried about having the stomach to follow through with it. Her misgivings about slaughtering the beast had all evaporated, replaced with a slight, yet undeniable, thirst for blood. As soon as her nephew returned from his dinner to pick up little Julia, she would get down to business without delay. But first she needed to pop out and find a suitable plastic mat before the stores all closed for the night. If she left now, she knew she could make it over to the housewares store on First Ave before it closed.

With some misgivings, she decided it would be better to just leave the child alone in her apartment for a few minutes, especially since tearing her away from her favorite show would not be an easy or pleasant task. Besides which, shopping with little Julia was always a nightmare. She always demanded that her auntie purchase whatever glittery object caught her eye, and if she refused, there was a strong possibility of a meltdown.

Julia was a pretty child, but strong-willed and precocious. Mrs. Butler would have preferred a niece who was well-mannered and obedient. But she realized those kinds of girls were in short supply in today's world. She consoled herself with the hope that, once she was older, her niece would be well served in life by the Butler determination. Although so far tonight, she had no complaints—little Julia had been a perfect little TV-watching zombie.

Mrs. Butler slipped the knife and the honing rod back

into the butcher block. Grabbing her purse and slipping on her shoes, she called out to her niece:

"Sweetie. Auntie needs to go down to the laundry room. I'll be back in a few minutes. Just sit tight and don't answer the phone or the door! Okay?" It was better to tell her a little fib, so her nephew wouldn't find out she had left his daughter all alone. Back when Mrs. Butler had been a young girl, just a little older than Julia was now, she had often been left to look after herself and her younger sister for days at a time and was expected to do the cleaning and the cooking to boot. And nobody had ever thought twice about it. But they just didn't raise kids that way anymore.

Her niece took no notice of her whatsoever as she stepped out the front door, pulling her trusty shopping cart behind her. The door closed with a click, and she stood motionless in the hallway for a moment, listening. Reassured that the only sounds were coming from the television, she turned and made her way down the hall.

28. PIRATE

[7:15 p.m.]

I f he needed proof that things could always be worse, then being dragged into the closet and having the door slammed shut removed all doubt. The tiniest amount of light seeped under the door, and his eyes quickly adjusted to pick out the fuzzy outlines of fur coats hanging on the rod above his head. An intense and repulsive smell added to his distress. Not even the strong smell of feet and leather coming from the neatly arranged shoe rack next to him could mask the pungent odor coming from the pockets of the garments overhead. It made him even more miserable.

Pirate had to admit he was feeling sorry for himself. One moment he had been a cheerful cat, enjoying an evening prowl in his own backyard. And the next he had been neatly trapped in a cage by a hideous old woman. This had offended him on many levels. For starters he knew he was smarter than that. His alarm bells had been ringing like mad as he'd tiptoed into the open cage. But of course, he had ignored them, drawn onward by the enchanting smell of catnip. Damn catnip! It was his one weakness in life. He simply couldn't trust himself around the stuff. Which was why he had been so easily led down the path to disaster.

Out of all the indignities he had been subjected to, being outsmarted by the old woman was what bothered him the most. He had always considered humans to be relatively dim-witted creatures, constantly running around all over the place, never taking the time to enjoy the simple pleasures of life. And yet, he, the great garden explorer, had been hunted and caught like a blind week-old kitten. And now he was completely helpless. He knew the old lady was just trying to figure out how to finish him off. He could smell it on her. She was clearly deranged—talking to herself and staring into space as if she were seeing things that weren't there. Obviously, he had fallen into the hands of a whacko cat killer. Just his luck.

Well, whatever she had in mind, he wouldn't make it easy for her, that's for sure. If she thought it was a simple task to kill a cat, let alone a cat like him, she was in for a nasty surprise. Overcome by a sudden urge for retribution, Pirate reached through the bars up to the coats above him and raked them with his claws.

He snagged a nearby mink sheathed in a plastic cover and tore into it angrily. When he had shredded the bottom of that coat, he moved on to its neighbor, and then did one more for good measure. He could feel the animalness of these hides. They were probably trophy kills from the human murderess.

Perhaps she meant to turn his own skin into a morbid decorative collar. The thought made all the hairs on his tail stand on end.

When he was satisfied with his work ripping up the coats, he squatted down in a corner of the cage and urinated on the closet floor. The smell of his urine helped a little with the strange closet smell, but not much.

But these small measures were far from the solution he needed to his situation. He simply had to get out of this cage soon, or it would be too late. The hunger in his belly was getting hard to ignore. He decided it was time for another round of loud yowling. The sound would not carry very far, enclosed in this small space, deadened by the coats above him. But she must have thrown him in here for a reason. He'd heard the sound of the front door opening and closing a couple of times, and the voice of a small child talking to his tormentor, followed by the sound of a television. Another quieter click that could have been the front door again had not escaped his sharp ears. And now all that was left was the noise from the TV set. Yes, given his few options it was definitely time for another bout of caterwauling.

The gnawing hunger in his gut fueled his rage, and he used this fury to amplify his naturally loud calls to their full resonant power. He kept it up as if his life depended on it.

As he meowed his lungs out, Pirate wondered what Ollie was up to at that moment. Was he searching for him? Was there any hope of being rescued by his dear friend? An outside chance perhaps, but he wouldn't bet on it. Pirate was aware of Ollie's considerable limitations. He had no sense of smell, terrible hearing, and absolutely no talent for stealth. You could hear him clomping around in his boots from a mile away. With all their glaring shortcomings, it was a mystery how humans managed to stay alive. Surely it had something to do with the strange backward toes humans had on their front paws? This peculiarity gave them their amazing ability to hold things, open boxes and doors, and build things like cages. Pirate knew that if only he had some backwards toes, he would be out of this cage so fast he would be nothing but a blur.

He was about to give up on his latest spell of noisemaking when the door was suddenly flung open. His eyes adjusted quickly to the bright light. A young blond child stood there staring into the closet. She took a step back in surprise when she saw him crouched in his cage.

"Meaow," he said sweetly.

"A kitty! There's a kitty in the closet!" The girl squatted and took a close look at him. He looked back at her with pleading eyes.

"Meaow," he repeated softly.

"Oh no! Kitty is locked in a cage. Poor kitty." Her little hands reached out and fumbled with the latch while Pirate continued to meow imploringly. After a brief struggle, it clicked open and she lifted up the cage door.

29. OLLIE

[7:35 p.m.]

Ollie and Zara were standing on the corner of Fifth Street and Avenue A. They were waiting for Cassandra, the girl from the voicemail. On the phone, this friendly neighbor had sketched out the disturbing scene she'd witnessed outside her window the night before. She'd told them about the yowling cat, about her view through the telescope, and about the old woman who had dragged a cage indoors. Both Ollie and Zara were left dumbfounded by her story. Cassandra had sympathized with their shock, and very kindly offered to help them track down this fiendish catnapper.

They'd been waiting for her for about ten minutes, during which time Ollie kept thinking about poor Pirate trapped in a cage. And the more he thought about this, the angrier he got. "What would make someone do such a thing?" he sputtered indignantly. "The woman must be insane. Old lady or not, she's gonna regret trapping Pirate when I catch up with her."

"Now let's not do anything stupid," Zara said, giving him a stern look.

"If I hadn't had my headphones on last night, I probably would have heard all the commotion outside," Ollie said ruefully.

"Look on the bright side. At least Pirate wasn't vaporized by an alien life-form."

"I guess that's true. But I was right that something strange had happened to him."

"You were definitely right about that."

Just then a slender young woman with dark brown hair came hurrying down the sidewalk and looked their way questioningly. She was wearing a green sundress and tan cowboy boots, and she had a wide-eyed ingenue look about her.

"Are you Cassandra?" he asked her.

"Yes. You must be Oliver?"

"Call me Ollie. And this is my friend Zara. Thanks so much for your help. It really means a lot."

They chatted for a few minutes as they hashed out a rough plan. Ollie warmed to Cassandra quickly. He could tell Zara approved of her too. Ollie mentioned that he would happily pay her the reward in cash once they found Pirate.

"Oh, I don't need a reward," Cassandra said dismissively. "I mean, I'm not rich or anything, don't get me wrong—I'm an aspiring actress—but, yeah, keep your money."

"Wait? Are you sure?" Ollie stared at her in amazement.

"Yes, of course. I love animals. And it's the neighborly

thing to do. Should we get going? I'm sure you're eager to track down your poor cat as soon as possible."

"Do you guys think that maybe the local precinct should be our first stop?" Zara suggested hesitantly.

"I tried calling the cops last night." Cassandra told them about how she was transferred to animal control, and how they had disabused her of the notion that the old woman's actions would be viewed with suspicion by the authorities.

"Then I guess we have no choice but to confront her ourselves," Zara said regretfully.

"You're pretty sure you can figure out what building she is in, right?" Ollie asked.

"The facades look very different from the back of the buildings, but I should be able to narrow it down to one or two entrances. Then we can just ring some buzzers and hope someone lets us in."

"Ollie," said Zara, "if we find this woman, you should let me do the talking."

"I'm not making any promises," Ollie growled.

The three of them headed south along Avenue A, the two girls walking shoulder to shoulder on the narrow sidewalk, chatting airily, with Ollie trailing behind them. A siren wailed in the distance. Traffic and pedestrians were sparse in the vicinity at the moment. They made it about a hundred feet further down the block when Cassandra stopped short. Her gaze was locked on a gray-haired woman pulling a shopping cart, who was scurrying across Avenue A. To Ollie and Zara, she was just another random passerby, but Cassandra was staring at her intently.

"Hey guys, look over there!" said Cassandra. "I may be

wrong, but I think that woman crossing the street might be the crazy old lady herself. I'm not completely sure, but when she turned her head I got a good look at her face, and I could swear it's the same person. She's got the same deranged expression."

Ollie became alert. "You think that's her? Quick, let's catch up!"

The trio broke into a sprint, but the surprisingly spry woman had turned up some steps and was opening an entranceway door with a key. Before they could even call out, she'd disappeared from sight, and the door had swung shut behind her. They made a mad dash to the entrance, but when they got to the building's steps, the woman was nowhere to be seen.

30. MRS. BUTLER

[7:40 p.m.]

Mrs. Butler hurried down the long hallway toward her front door. Her excursion had taken longer than expected, and it had been about twenty minutes in all since she'd left her godchild all alone.

Even more distressing were the many lost cat flyers she had passed on her way to and from the shop. She'd discovered one on the lamppost outside of her very own building and another pinned in the entrance to the housewares store. Everywhere she turned, she saw the pink flyer bemoaning that damned cat. Clearly that young man from the fire escape was turning the neighborhood upside down trying to locate his missing pet. The 150-dollar reward seemed incredible to her. Why on earth would anyone pay that much for a mangy furball? Well, she would be saving the young man some cash at any rate.

When she stepped into her apartment, she was alarmed to see little Julia just standing in the foyer waiting for her, smiling broadly and looking pleased with herself. Her grand-niece looked no worse for the wear, thank goodness. The television was still on in the background, but the cartoons had been replaced by a cooking show.

"Auntie, I found a big kitty in the closet!" Julia's angelic face was beaming with excitement.

"What? No! Tell me you didn't open the closet, child!" snapped Mrs. Butler.

"I did! He was right in there," she pointed to the coat closet, and Mrs. Butler saw that the door had been thrown wide open. "He was in a cage. Poor thing. But I rescued him!" she looked up into her godmother's face with shining eyes, clearly expecting to be praised for her good deed.

"God help us," said Mrs. Butler, looking around wildly. "You didn't really set that beast loose, did you?" The child nodded happily. Striding over to the closet, Mrs. Butler peered down at the cage on the floor. She gasped. It was indeed empty.

"Oh my Lord! Where is he? Where did he go?" she shrieked, clutching her godchild by the shoulders.

"Auntie! You're hurting me!" she whimpered. "He is over there, under the table." She pointed into the dining room.

Sure enough, the hulking brute was crouched in the shadows under her table, glaring at her, ears flattened and lips curled back. A jolt of fear shot through her. Freed from his cage, not having eaten for a whole day, the enormous tomcat was terrifying.

Conflicting emotions gripped Nora Butler. Had she finally lost her fight against this wretched animal? Should she raise the white flag and just open the patio door and try and shoo him back outside? Were they in actual danger? She stared at the cat, who met her own gaze unwaveringly, his narrow eyes filled with venom. But he made no move in their direction and seemed to be biding his time.

Little Julia had stopped pouting about the way Auntie had grabbed her, and Mrs. Butler was shocked to realize she was making a beeline for the dining room table.

"Pretty kitty!" said her grandniece in a high-pitched voice.

"Julia, don't go near that cat!" screamed Mrs. Butler in a panic. She started forward to grab her niece, but it was too late as the child was already approaching the animal. Bending down, the girl reached out and patted the cat on the head. Much to Mrs. Butler's amazement, the cat ignored the girl's attentions, its eyes never veering from his captor's face. Breathing a sigh of relief, Mrs. Butler decided she needed to formulate a new plan.

Racking her brain, she came up with a quick strategy that might just allow her to snatch victory from the jaws of defeat. She would do what she should have done from the beginning and just cut the beast to pieces with the colonel's sword. It would be a fitting end for the creature. And she would then tell people that the animal had broken into her apartment and attacked them. She could play the role of the hero who had saved her niece from a rabid stray. A little baking soda sprinkled on the dead animal's lips would help sell the story.

Moving slowly, she edged her way over to where the civil war cutlass hung on the living room wall, careful not to turn her back on the now growling animal. Inching her way closer and closer, she made it to the wall. She reached up and slowly lifted the sword off the brackets. The cat watched her suspiciously as she slowly drew the blade and tossed the empty scabbard down on the lowboy.

"Julia, come away from there, child, that animal is dangerous!" she commanded, but her niece paid her no heed whatsoever.

The animal's attention had wandered. She followed its gaze and saw that it was staring at the apartment door—which she had thoughtlessly left ajar. Mrs Butler's eyes widened with alarm—*oh no you don't, you demon cat!*

They were both about the same distance from the front door, and with a slight head start, Mrs. Butler made a mad dash for it, sword in hand. After a moment's hesitation, the cat sprung to life, racing her to the exit. Mrs. Butler's seventy-year-old legs had not been asked to run for many years, while the cat covered the ground in an instant. But pumped full of adrenaline, she managed to get within striking distance of the animal before it reached freedom, so she put her whole arm into a wild swinging blow. The cat, seeing the blade descending toward him out of the corner of his eye, stopped short, nails digging into the oriental carpet, and the blade cut through the air, passing just in front of him and banging into the floor. The jolt was enough to send the blade jumping out of her hand and make her arm instantly numb. The beast dodged the now airborne sword, and, with lightning speed, turned and sunk his teeth deep into Mrs. Butler's calf, wrapping his claws around her leg. She shrieked in pain. The cat quickly let go and dashed off, slipping through the door's narrow opening and out into the hallway. Mrs. Butler stood there, clutching her bleeding leg.

She took stock of her wounded leg and her tingling arm. She breathed in deeply and shook off any nagging doubts. She wasn't done yet. She would show that feline that the Butlers were made of stern stuff. That she could rise to the challenge in the heat of battle. She snatched up the sword from where it had fallen and followed the cat out the door. If she hurried, she could corral the creature in the hallway and take another swipe at him. This time she wouldn't miss. A feverish white haze had settled over her eyes, as all thoughts other than killing that critter were pushed from her mind. She limped down the hallway toward the building entrance, but there was no sign of the cat anywhere. The building's doors were still closed, and through the glass-paneled doors, she saw three figures huddled outside the building looking at her with astonishment. One of them struck her as vaguely familiar. For a second she wondered what she must look like to these people, disheveled and with a cutlass in her hand. But she was beyond caring anymore. Turning on her heels, she retraced her steps toward the building's stairs. The only other direction the wicked animal could have gone was up.

Julia poked her head out of the apartment and seemed astonished by the sight of her bleeding, sword wielding Auntie marching by. "Please don't hurt kitty, Auntie!" she begged. But Mrs. Butler didn't spare her niece a second glance. She stopped at the bottom of the stairs, stuck her head over the banister, and looked up. Reflective demon eyes glared down at her from one flight up.

Gathering the skirts of her dress with her free hand, Mrs. Butler charged up the staircase, sword in hand.

31. OLLIE

[7:40 p.m.]

Ollie stood huddled in the entranceway with Zara and Cassandra. They studied the numbers and labels on the intercom. It appeared there were six ground floor apartments. Cassandra suggested they avoid 1B, which had a black punch type label with the word "super" written on it.

They pressed a random button on one of the upper floors in the hopes that someone would buzz them in. A gruff voice demanded to know who they were and what they wanted. They didn't reply, shrugging at each other silently as they tried a different button on another floor. There was no reply. Another buzzer. More silence.

They were about to try their luck with another random apartment when they were startled by the appearance of a bizarre figure rushing into the building's lobby. It was an old woman who was clutching a long, curved sword in her bony hand. Her eyes were frantic and her gray hair swirled around her face. They stared at her in disbelief. Ollie quickly put two and two together and realized that this lunatic must be the person they'd come here to find. The woman was looking around herself desperately. She glanced their way for a second, and then spun around and disappeared back in the direction she'd come from.

"I have no idea what's going on, but that lady with the sword is our catnapper," Cassandra said, pointing into the building. "For the record, I did tell you she was crazy."

"Yeah, you weren't kidding," said Zara. "Is it just me, or did it look as if she was chasing something? You don't think . . . ?"

Ollie reached over to the intercom and jammed half a dozen buttons. Seconds later the doors buzzed loudly, and they pushed through into the building's lobby. They took off down a pale marble hallway, in the direction the woman had disappeared, with Ollie in the lead. The apartment doors they passed were all closed and quiet until they turned a corner and came across a young girl standing in an open doorway, an unhappy look on her face.

"Hello, sweetie," Zara said, bending down to the child's height, "we are looking for our lost cat. Have you seen him by any chance?"

"Auntie chased the big kitty upstairs!" said the girl, pointing up the staircase. From somewhere way up above them, they heard the sound of echoing footsteps. Zara thanked her and exchanged a worried look with Ollie. They hurried off in pursuit.

"Er . . . is that blood?" Cassandra asked, pointing to a trail of red droplets on the steps.

"I think we'd better speed up," Zara said. Ollie was already racing up the stairs.

"You two should probably just wait downstairs," Ollie called over his shoulder to them. "He's my cat. I'm the only one who needs to stick his neck out. When I asked you guys for help, we didn't factor in a deranged lady with a sword."

"Don't be ridiculous," said Zara. "You're not leaving me behind."

"I'm not frightened by that ugly old woman either," Cassandra declared boldly, "sword or no sword."

Ollie glanced back at the two brave-faces rushing up the stairs behind him. He was too incensed to be worried about his own safety, but the thought of either of them getting hurt made him apprehensive.

By the time they got to the sixth floor, Ollie was breathing heavily. He considered himself in decent shape from taking the stairs daily in his own building. But he had to slow down a bit and try to catch his breath for the last few flights. The elevator might have been a better idea, but he couldn't know what floor the woman might turn off onto. He could still hear the old lady's clicking footsteps above them, and he guessed she could hear them clomping up the stairs behind her. A curious thought occurred to him as he passed the seventh floor—Miss Ruby had been right about everything so far. If this old lady with the sword didn't qualify as a malevolent force, then he didn't know what did.

32. MRS. BUTLER

[7:50 p.m.]

Mrs. Butler felt like her lungs were on fire by the time she reached the top floor. She was in great shape for a septuagenarian, thanks to her frequent birding excursions. But at her age, no one was built for running up nine flights of stairs, and she had felt each successive step in her knees as well as her lungs. But she'd been propelled upward relentlessly by one clear thought—killing that beastly animal. Reaching the top floor, she heard the critter above her scratching against the closed door to the roof. A smile played on her face. This was the end of the road for him—there was nowhere left to run.

She took the last set of stairs more slowly, trying to recover some of her breath for the final confrontation. She saw the cat's head poke out through the staircase railing once again, its yellow eyes menacing and defiant. The savage creature had bitten her once already and raked her with its claws. She didn't intend to let that happen again. If she got close enough, she was just going to skewer him like a shish kebab. She advanced stealthily, her sword arm stretched out ahead of her.

As she approached the uppermost landing, she was flabbergasted to see the cat hop onto its back feet and reach up to lean its front paws on the bar across the door. She heard a click and the door cracked open. Without a backward glance, the animal butted the door open further with his head and slipped through the resulting crack out onto the roof.

"Dammit to hell! I will cut you to pieces, you demon cat, if it's the last thing I do!" she spat, running up the last few steps and barreling through the doorway. Charging out onto the roof, she slammed the door shut behind her. There would be no escape for him in that direction.

She found the roof bare except for two large water towers. The cat had slunk over to the closer of the two, in the middle of the roof, and was crouching behind one of the structure's steel legs.

"Say your prayers, you blasted creature," Mrs. Butler muttered gleefully.

She approached slowly, and the cat backed away hissing. His fur was all puffed out, making him seem even bigger than he was. The water tower cast deep shadows on the rooftop. Instinct carried the black-and-white cat deeper into the darkness beneath it. But she could still see his yellow eyes and patches of white fur, so she crept slowly forward, determined not to spook him before she got within striking distance. Inching onward she closed the gap with the retreating animal, until she was only about six feet away, standing in the space directly under the middle water tower. The fiendish animal hissed at her again and made swiping motions with his paws at her outstretched sword.

She counted to three, girding herself for a sudden lunge. But just as she was about to make a stab, she heard a strange buzzing coming from the water tower above her. Glancing up, she saw what looked like a swarm of yellow lights descending upon her. She tried to step out of the way, but it was too late. These strange lights enveloped her, and in a moment of panic, she realized she could no longer move. The next thing she knew her feet had left the ground and she began to float slowly up toward the tower above, still clutching the colonel's weapon in her hand.

The cat was trapped by the lights, just as she was. It twisted and turned in the air as it was drawn up higher and higher toward the source of the light above.

Mrs. Butler struggled to wrap her brain around her current situation. Nothing in her long life had prepared her in any way for this moment, and she simply could not understand what was happening. She managed to turn her head upwards and saw that there was a round opening in the bottom of the tower that the lights were emitting from. Now twenty feet off the ground, she was horrified to realize that she was about to get sucked into the water tower itself. When her head broke the plane of the vessel the first thing she noticed in the dim light were rows of electronic controls. It occurred to her that she might be dreaming. But her leg still throbbed where the feral critter had bitten her, so she discarded that possibility.

As her eyes adjusted to the darkness, she was confronted

by a truly horrific sight. An impossibly large two-headed turtle was standing on two feet, close enough to reach out and touch her. The turtle's hideous heads both seemed to be glaring at her angrily. Again she told herself this must be some horrible nightmare. But if that was the case, she couldn't seem to wake up. She continued to be guided by the light particles, which the giant turtle creature seemed to be controlling from a console.

The cat had also been drawn into the vessel and was hovering in mid air beside her, looking as unhappy and bewildered as she herself felt. They were separated by about three feet of space and drifting slowly apart. The turtle-like creature was holding a square silver device in one of its multiple hands, pointing it in her direction. A thin beam of blue light was emitting from the tip and scanning her from head to toe. Another of the thin green hands was holding a pointy metal gun-like device. The turtle creature looked very threatening. Mrs. Butler tried in vain to move her arms and legs, but it was like being trapped in thick jello. She could wriggle around, but she could not break free.

She found herself wafting closer to a large round chamber that looked like a hot tub with a glass lid. She had never felt so helpless in her whole life. She racked her brain for a way to escape. What would the colonel do? Surely he would've kept a trick or two up his sleeve? She closed her eyes and relaxed her body, letting herself go completely limp and no longer struggling against the yellow light, as she counted slowly to ten. Then, tightening her grip on her sword, she focused all her remaining energy into one sudden burst. Her arm broke free of the glow momentarily as she swung the sword at the turtle monster with all her might. The sword swished through the air toward one of the creature's necks. But it managed to raise an arm at the last second, and her cutlass clanged harmlessly against the strange instrument the giant turtle was holding.

The yellow light quickly recovered its hold on her and the strength seemed to have been dialed up a notch. Try as she might, she was unable to so much as twitch a finger. She was pleased to see that the creature had dropped the contraption it was holding. That was something at least. The beam slowly carried her over to the round tub, depositing her inside. To her horror, the transparent lid slid shut across the opening, sealing her in. The last sensation she felt before losing consciousness was the air in her lungs becoming intensely cold.

33. AXZLEPROVA

[7:50 p.m.]

AxzleProva had completed all their preparations. But even though it was already dark, they decided it would be best to wait until the general activity of the neighborhood died down. The primarily diurnal humans would soon commence their usual sleep cycles, at which point it would be much easier to slip away unnoticed.

They had resigned themselves to their mission's failure. It was regrettable, but they did their best to cope with this setback stoically. They resolved to take advantage of any upcoming downtime to pay a visit to their home planet, where a few weeks spent wallowing in their favorite swamp would serve as a much-needed restorative.

Just then, a flashing light on the main dashboard indicated that the protective wards they had set on the staircase had been breached for the second time that day. They exchanged concerned looks. This was serious—they had to assume that the local authorities had become involved. There was only one thing worse than being seen, and that was getting captured. Axzle immediately activated the ship's drive systems, while Prova disengaged the molecular anchors that were securing the ship to the rooftop.

Axzle's finger hovered over the liftoff lever as they stared at the screen showing the view of the rooftop entrance. Seconds later they were amazed to see none other than their favorite research subject—the giant black-and-white cat they had become so enchanted with—burst through the door. He came running straight toward their vessel and slunk into the shadows of one of the ship's legs.

But the cat was not alone. Close on his heels came a human female who they also recognized—the old woman who had foiled their research. She seemed enraged and was brandishing a primitive weapon. It was immediately apparent she was pursuing the feline with hostile intent. Axzle terminated the emergency liftoff with the flick of a switch.

"Looks like the cat managed to escape," said Prova. "But I think that woman intends to end its existence with that sharpened metal rod she is holding."

"I do believe you are right. All indications are that she is in attack mode. What hideous beasts these humans are."

"Indeed."

"Are we going to just sit here and do nothing while she terminates him?" Axzle asked.

"Interfering is way too risky," Prova responded tersely. "They are unaware of our presence, so it is imperative that we stay hidden."

"Well you might be able to live with the demise of that poor cat on your conscience, but I don't think I can. Look, she is chasing him into the path of our capture beam. We can have her immobilized and in our ship in seconds. Do a catch and release, just like before."

"That is a bad idea."

"No it is not," he insisted.

It would seem that they had reached their familiar stand-off. "Is this one of those moments where you are just going to do what you want anyway?"

"Yes, I think so, dearest shell-of-my-shell."

"Fine. Let's save that poor cat. But if it backfires, and we make it out of here in one piece, you should know I will be looking for a new shell-mate."

Axzle shot her a bemused smile and reached forward to toggle a few switches on the console. "Opening bay door and initiating beam capture!"

"I have to confess," said Prova, "that I have taken a strong personal dislike to this particular human."

"She is a truly revolting humanoid." He waited until the woman stepped right under their ship. "Activating light magnets now." Axzle spun a dial around quickly. Taken unawares, the woman was quickly enveloped, and the cat, who had made a sudden turn at the last moment, also found himself in the path of the beam. Both the human huntress and her prey were instantly immobilized and then drawn upward from the rooftop toward their ship. "Oops! Looks like we are going to make direct contact with the feline, after all. Less than ideal circumstances, I will admit. But maybe this is an opportunity for us to salvage our mission."

"I'm pretty sure that forcible capture is not the recommended method for initiating first contact with a new species," muttered Prova.

Once the old woman's head broke the perimeter of the vessel, Axzle switched to direct visual control. The human's face was contorted with anger and confusion about what was happening to her, but thankfully she did not think to cry out. Everything went smoothly up until the moment Prova was about to inject her with the sedative. With unforeseen strength and cunning, the human female momentarily broke free from the magnetic beam. Axzle barely had time to raise an arm to protect Prova from a vicious swipe of the human's primitive weapon. Thanks to his quick reflexes, the blow glanced off the bio scanner in his hand, leaving a startled Prova unharmed. The scare caused Prova to drop the intra-pulsar injector she was holding, and the sensitive tip snapped off when the device clanged into a control panel. They quickly regained full control of the subject and locked her hastily in the stasis chamber without bothering to sedate her first. Axzle breathed a sigh of relief. Close call.

They immediately turned their attention to the black-and-white cat floating in the yellow light in front of them. After watching him for so many weeks from afar, they felt a jolt of excitement to finally come face-to-face with the handsome feline. Unsurprisingly the poor cat looked aggrieved and desperate to reconnect its footing with something solid. They maneuvered the Earth cat to a nearby panel, and it seemed much relieved to put its weight on its own four paws.

"Once we return the cat to the surface, we should lift off immediately," Prova whispered. "I don't want to alarm you,

Axzle, but I have detected three human lifeforms observing us from the rooftop below. They snuck onto the roof when we were busy with the beam capture. Thankfully these newcomers appear to be local residents and are lacking in recording devices. One of them is the human male that this feline has subjugated."

Axzle acknowledged all this with a nod. Then he switched on the universal interpreter and turned to face their guest. He had no intention of passing up this opportunity for a quick interview.

"Greetings, Earth cat," Axzle said in a friendly tone. Strangled meows spewed from a speaker overhead. Hearing its own language, the feline looked even more mystified than before. Axzle bowed his head gently. "We come from another world. We mean you no harm and have rescued you from the clutches of this hideous human female." The translator spewed out more meows.

"Meaow," replied Pirate, no longer looking quite so panicked. A squishy blurp from the speaker above communicated his tentative thanks to his saviors, and they both twiddled their antennae back and forth madly, which was their species's equivalent of a smile. They were thrilled that communication had been established with positive early results.

"We are part of a great Amalgamation of interstellar beings. Perhaps someday you and your fellow Earth felines will join our great community?"

"Meaow meaow meaow meaow," said Pirate, by which he meant that he considered it doubtful. He pointed out that cats weren't really big joiners. He went on to request that they kindly return him to the roof as he had spotted his best friend as he was drifting up into their vessel, and was eager to be reunited with him.

AxzleProva muted the translator while they conferred with each other.

"How can it be?" Prova asked, perplexed. "That he considers the primitive human male a friend?"

"I do not know. And he does not quite grasp what a privilege it is to be considered for membership in the Amalgamation," Axzle added.

"Come to think of it," Prova mused, "it is not unusual for a symbiotic species to reject membership offers, unless they are extended to their symbionts as well!"

"Yes, that is correct," said Axzle. "I cannot believe we did not consider this possibility. Which means we either reject these felines as future members, or extend the invitation to the revolting humans."

"But humans are so utterly deplorable!" exclaimed Prova. "There is no way the committee would ever consider them for membership."

"Do you think that perhaps we may have misjudged humans?" asked Axzle. "Could some positive traits have been obscured by their very salient deficiencies?"

"The possibility never even occurred to me. I have trouble looking past their grotesque appearance," Prova confessed.

"Shell-mate, I think we need to make a trip down to the rooftop and meet this cat's friend. A brief interaction with these humans should clarify this question considerably."

Prova stared at him in disbelief. "Do you have mud for brains? We need to depart immediately. And I should not have to remind you that contact with humans has not been authorized. If we were foolish enough to reveal ourselves to these three humanoids, there is a good chance we will end up as a stuffed exhibit in one of their museums!"

"If we stay within the beam of light, it should shield us from any unexpected attacks," Azxle countered. "Humans have been flagged as potentially abhorrent, but they haven't been blacklisted yet. A benign interaction, justified by their symbiotic relationship to our assigned species, could push the humanoids into a more favorable status within the Amalgamation. This would be a major accomplishment for our mission."

"Oh shells! Why do you keep diving into the deep end of the swamp?" Prova wondered if this was what it felt like to be a criminal. Step by step, her partner had led her down the path toward going rogue. She had lost track of how many regulations they had broken. Their meticulous research project, which had been going so smoothly only a day earlier, had veered into uncharted territory.

As usual, once Axzle got hold of an idea, he refused to let it go. Not having the time for a protracted argument, she gave in to him once more. Even though she was utterly terrified that this latest scheme would get them killed. Axzle explained to the feline that they wanted to pop down to the surface and meet his friend. The cat meowed to say that he thought this was a fantastic idea and that they would like Ollie. AxzleProva quickly strapped on the necessary gear. Then, holding the purring cat in their arms, they stepped into the beam of light.

34. OLLIE

[7:50 p.m.]

asping for air, Ollie struggled up the last flight of stairs to the roof, the two girls close on his heels. They were all breathing heavily, but they'd managed to close the gap somewhat with the old woman. Enough for him to catch a glimpse of her feet above him, followed by the loud clunk of the roof door opening and closing.

Moments later, standing in front of that door, Ollie stopped to catch his breath. Then he pushed it open, and leaped through the exit. All three of them spilled out into the open air. He expected to come face-to-face with a sword-wielding lunatic and was ready for anything. But as it turned out, none of them were really prepared for the scene that was playing out in front of them on the rooftop.

Standing before them was the large metal water tower, flickering yellow lights radiating from an opening in its underbelly. Suspended in the air below the tower, bathed in the warm glow, were both the sword-clutching old woman and a large black-and-white cat—Pirate.

Ollie and his friends stood frozen in place, eyes popping out of their heads and jaws slack as they watched both the woman and the cat drift slowly up towards the underside of the tower. The figures floated into the glowing gap, and they watched as a shaggy tail, followed by two human legs, receded into the metal vessel. The woman's feet were kicking about wildly as they vanished into the interior, and one foot caught the edge of the tank. A black leather shoe was knocked loose, falling down to the rooftop.

Ollie exchanged astonished looks with his two companions.

"Do you still think I'm crazy?" Ollie asked Zara without taking his eyes from the tower. "I don't see any wires, do you?"

"I can't believe what I'm seeing," Zara gasped. "Is this a hallucination?"

"If you're hallucinating, then so am I," Cassandra said falteringly.

"The water tower is clearly some sort of spaceship," Ollie pointed out matter-of-factly.

"I'm sorry," said Zara, "but spaceships don't land on New York City rooftops. They just don't!"

But Ollie, who'd had all day to wrap his mind around this, was having no trouble believing his own eyes. He was less concerned with the extraterrestrial aspects of the situation, and more preoccupied about his very terrestrial cat. He could accept that aliens might have traveled from god knows where to pop down for a visit. But as far as he was concerned, neither the great distance they had traveled, nor their unfamiliarity with local customs in any way excused their abducting his cat. He objected to their actions in the strongest possible terms.

He wasn't sure why Pirate seemed to be attracting so many kidnappers these days, but he didn't like it one bit. He didn't like it when crazy old ladies trapped him in a cage. And he didn't like it when beings from another planet used a freaking tractor beam to suck him up into their ship.

Ollie and his two friends inched a little closer and peered up into the light. But they could make out nothing more than a haze of yellow. They stood there staring upward, at a loss for what to do next.

"Holy smokes," Cassandra exclaimed. "What I wouldn't give to have my camera with me."

"But—but—but," stammered Zara. "We must have stumbled onto a movie set or something."

"If this was a movie set,' said Ollie, "there'd be a bunch of people standing around looking bored. And there would be some guy with a headset telling us we can't stand here. So I'm pretty sure what we're witnessing is an actual alien abduction. The real deal. And poor Pirate seems to be one of the victims."

They stood there gaping at the water tower wordlessly. Ollie couldn't believe his cat had just been sucked into a spaceship. Was it up to him to rescue his furry friend from these intergalactic abductors? Thinking about poor Pirate being terrorized inside the water tower made him angry, and he knew he couldn't stand there and do nothing. He had to at least try.

"You guys hang tight, I'm gonna climb up that ladder there and see if I can't poke my head inside and let them know how I feel about them running off with my cat."

Ollie took a step forward, but Zara quickly grabbed hold of his arm. "Ollie! What are you thinking? It's way too dangerous!"

"Look, Zara, I came up here to save my cat and that's just what I plan on doing."

"But . . . this is crazy!" Zara seemed close to freaking out.

"I'm sorry, but there's no way I'm going to stand around and do nothing while he gets abducted."

Ollie pulled free of her grasp and took half a step toward the ladder when he stopped short. Something was emerging from the tower. It descended slowly in the glowing light, and he soon recognized the scaly feet as belonging to the creature he'd seen earlier in the day. His mind flashed to the ray gun that had vaporized the pigeon this morning. He glanced nervously at the two girls, trying to hide the current of fear shooting through him. They looked rattled as well, but were still rooted to the spot, curiosity winning out over both fear and common sense.

The alien had emerged into full view, and Ollie was relieved to see it didn't seem to be holding anything that looked like a gun. Although it held a square gizmo in one of its four hands. Even more unbelievably, he recognized Pirate's shaggy outline cradled in their long skinny arms. Pirate was looking right at him and seemed reassuringly happy and alert. Ollie knew Pirate wasn't the sort of cat who would let just anyone pick him up. Moments later the alien's two feet were on solid ground, its two heads swiveled toward the three of them, and its yellow eyes seemed to be looking right at him.

Ollie realized he was trembling slightly. But even if he'd wanted to run, his legs felt like rubber. He kept looking from the alien faces to Pirate, and then back again. Wordlessly the giant space turtle advanced toward them, coming to a halt a few feet away. Up close, Ollie could see how leathery its skin was, making out faint splotches of darker green. The two heads were actually different. One of them had slightly larger eyes and more defined cheekbones, and seemed to him to have a more hostile expression.

The head on the left, the friendlier one, opened its mouth and made a strange chittering sound. Then a monotone voice emanated from the boxy device the creature was holding in one of its four hands: "Greetings, Earthlings. We mean you no harm. We are escorting your friend safely to you."

The extraterrestrial lifted its arms, holding Pirate out to him. Mustering his courage, Ollie tottered forward and took the cat from the extraterrestrial's outstretched hands. Pirate looked up at him and meowed happily.

It was Cassandra who first found her voice. "Greetings. Welcome to planet Earth," she said boldly to the creature. The device they were holding took their words and transformed them into the peculiar chittering sounds.

"Yes. Welcome," croaked Ollie nervously. "And thanks for returning my cat to me safely. I was very worried."

There was more chittering directed their way, this time

from the other head, whose expression seemed more guarded than its twin's. "It is an honor to meet the distinguished friends of this amazing feline. Unfortunately, we cannot stay to acquaint ourselves better. We must depart from your lovely planet now. Farewell to you all."

"What happened to the old woman," Zara asked urgently.

"We have detained the old human female temporarily to prevent injury to your four-legged friend. We will release her some distance away, where she won't be an immediate threat to anyone."

"Thanks," said Ollie. And he meant it.

The alien walked backward until it was back under its ship. The warm yellow light appeared again, and the creature drifted up into its vessel.

Ollie looked down at the heavy cat squirming in his arms. His furry friend was very much alive, looking up at him with those bright yellow eyes. Ollie planted a big old kiss on his forehead.

"Okay. Well we got Pirate back, that's good," said Zara. "And we didn't get abducted or vaporized. Do you think maybe it's time we got the heck out of here?"

Just then, the yellow light above them winked out and the spherical opening in the bottom of the tower slid closed with a *snick*. With Pirate wrapped in his arms, Ollie took a step closer to the roof entrance, his friends moving in unison. They froze again, wide-eyed, when all four of the tower's legs retracted silently into the barrel, and the railing and ladders on the side of the tower flipped inside out, replaced by smooth silver panels. What was left was a gleaming silver cone, bobbing in the sky above them.

Then the city lights around them winked out, plunging the roof into blackness. They became aware of the sputtering sound of a helicopter nearby, the whir of the blades cutting through the air growing louder as it drew closer. A spotlight pierced the darkness, aimed at the hovering spaceship. A second searchlight from a different chopper appeared on the other side. It was difficult to make out what happened next, but there was a loud *whoosh,* and when the surrounding lights came back on moments later, the alien ship was nowhere to be seen. The helicopters were still hovering overhead, their searchlights scanning the rooftop madly.

"Okay, that was just insane," Zara declared. She had a dazed look about her. As if she had blown a fuse somewhere in her mind.

Cassandra was shaking her head, trying to clear the cobwebs too. "Dad will never believe it," she muttered under her breath. "How do I even begin to explain that I just met a real-life alien on a New York rooftop?"

"That was nice of them to bring Pirate back down," Ollie said happily.

"I guess," said Cassandra. "But they basically abducted the old lady."

"I'm not sure it counts if it's a sword-wielding lunatic," Ollie replied. "They were performing a public service, really."

Cassandra was still staring up into the sky, searching the heavens for some evidence of their recent encounter. "I feel like I'm in a dream."

"Hey, let's get out of here," Ollie suggested. Pirate was squirming in his arms, wanting to be put down, but Ollie kept a tight hold on him.

"Good idea," Zara agreed. "Just in case that creature changes its mind and decides to return and pick up some more passengers."

Suddenly, the door to the rooftop burst open. A dozen helmeted figures swarmed onto the roof. They were dressed in black body armor and were carrying frighteningly large guns. Some of them were wearing night vision goggles. The men surrounded them and someone barked an order at them to not move a muscle. Petrified, Ollie and his two friends stood still as statues. A man in a dark gray suit emerged onto the roof next, looking very much like the person in charge. He had slicked-back hair and a heavily creased forehead. He strode over to them and grimaced as he looked the three of them up and down.

"They are scanning as three humans and one cat," proclaimed one of the men who was waving a wand around them.

"Bystanders then. My favorite." The guy in the suit dismissed his men with a gesture and stood there eyeing them like they were a headache he would rather not deal with.

"Here's the deal, I'm not going to introduce myself. But I'm a federal agent. That's all you need to know. Now tell me what it is you think you saw?" he demanded brusquely.

Zara gave him the gist of everything they'd witnessed since stepping out onto the roof. Ollie chimed in here and there with a few details. This brush with the authorities made him more jumpy than the alien encounter. But at least no one was pointing guns their way anymore. One of the squad members interrupted them to show his boss an object they'd discovered on the rooftop, which he was holding in a shiny metallic clamp. Ollie identified it for them as the old lady's shoe. The agent in charge narrowed his eyes and instructed his underling to bag it.

"You say she lived in one of the ground floor apartments?"

Ollie and the girls nodded.

"Listen, guys. I've got one unidentified flying object and one missing person. Both of which should be easy to process. It seems like an isolated incident, and I don't want it to get blown out of proportion. The public could easily freak out if they start hearing about unidentified flying objects and abductions in a major city. If we're not careful, the press will get a hold of this story, and that in turn could lead to hysteria in the general populace. Suffice it to say that my job is to keep all that from happening. Panic prevention, you might call it. So the last thing I need is three witnesses blabbing their mouths and putting ideas into people's heads. This will go a lot easier for all of us if you three can pretend like this never happened. You don't want me to drag you down to the field office for questioning, and I don't want to have to do a pile of paperwork. So can we just agree that you saw a few strange lights in the sky and some helicopters?"

"I didn't see a darn thing," Ollie declared.

"Me neither," Zara said quickly.

"I don't think I even had my eyes open," Cassandra added.

"Glad to hear it." The man in the suit leaned in and whispered confidentially: "Just between us, no one would ever believe you, anyway. Trust me, I know." He straightened his tie. "Now—get the hell off my roof."

35. MANOLO

[one week later]

Natalya had prepared a feast of fried fish with plantains for Saturday lunch. Manolo was feeling pleasantly stuffed as he pushed back from the table and let out a loud burp.

"Manolo! Please," exclaimed his sister, who was sitting across from him, along with her husband, Paul. "I hope you behaved with more refinement at that job interview the other day."

"Don't worry, I was super presentable. You should have seen me, all clean-shaven in my new suit. Natalya even took me to get a manicure at her nail place." The truth was Manolo had barely recognized himself in the mirror.

A smiling Natalya finished clearing the table and announced she was going to step out and grab the mail from the box in the lobby. Paul shuffled over to the sofa where he looked about ready to pass out from overeating. Manolo had been waiting for just such an opportunity to catch his sister alone, and he quickly pulled her into the kitchen.

"What do you think?" he asked her in a hushed voice.

"It's totally weird. She's like a completely different person," Maricela replied, shaking her head. "If I wasn't seeing it with my own eyes, I wouldn't believe it."

"I know, right?"

"So is she always like this? Or is it on and off?"

"All the time. Ever since, you know—our little ceremony last week."

"Wow. I'll be honest with you, I thought the whole candle thing might help a little, but this—this is on a completely different level."

"Exactly. It's freaking me out," said Manolo, "but mostly I'm just afraid that it won't last."

"You know, she cornered me earlier and told me she hoped we could let bygones be bygones and start fresh."

"I'm not surprised. It was her idea to invite you guys over for lunch."

"Really? Wow, I think it's for real, little bro. I hope for your sake, and for mine, that it's permanent."

"Is that all you can think to say?"

"The candle worked?" said Maricela with a giggle.

"C'mon, get real, how could lighting a candle do this?"

"Don't forget about the necklace and the cactus. The Lady of the Shadows works in mysterious ways."

"Be serious, Maricela, please, I'm freaking out. It's like waking up and finding out the last three years of my life were just a bad dream."

"I think I may go have a chat with Rosa and light a few candles myself. I mean, Paul is great, but he's no Natalya."

"Stop joking around—I need to know if this is really happening or not."

"Pinch yourself. If you don't wake up, then assume you're good. Have you noticed anything else strange about her behavior?"

"No, not really. Although the other night, we were watching TV. and a trailer for that new movie *Mars Attacks* came on. Natalya freaked out! She just shot up out of her chair and ran into the bedroom. I followed her in to make sure she was okay, and I found her hiding under the bed."

"That's pretty odd."

"Yeah. Although some pretty odd things have been happening around here lately. Did I tell you federal agents swarmed the building last week? I'm not sure what they were looking for. They were very tight-lipped. My best guess is it was a failed drug bust or something."

The sound of the front door opening and closing let them know Natalya had returned with the mail. Moments later she popped into the kitchen in search of them and found Maricela busy washing the dishes while Manolo dried.

"Oh, please, Maricela, don't worry about the dishes, you are a guest in our home. Just go and make yourself comfortable in the living room while I take care of this mess."

"Nonsense, it's the least I can do after that wonderful meal. You cooked, so you get to put your feet up. The chef always gets a free pass on clean up!"

"How about we all do them together," said Natalya.

"We'll get it done sooner, and then we can relax. Maybe play a game of dominos?"

"I love dominos!" exclaimed Maricela. "How have we never played together before?"

Manolo furiously polished the spots out of a stem glass, his brow deeply furrowed as he attempted once more to puzzle out the events of the past week. He had been worried his sister would burst his bubble and tell him he was being played for a fool. But instead she seemed as taken with the new Natalya as he was.

In just one week, she was utterly transformed. The smile that frequently lit up her face was the most jarring change, as it was the polar opposite of the scowl that had been a fixture for so long. Manolo found himself smiling more too.

It didn't stop there. She had started cooking dinner every night, dusting off Aunt Rita's recipe box. And she had sold all her fancy jewelry, and put the money she got for it into a joint bank account—to save up for the honeymoon they'd never had. She hoped that by cutting back on unnecessary luxuries, that they would have enough for ten days at a nice hotel in Aruba by the spring. Manolo was already picturing himself on a white sand beach with a tropical drink in his hand.

She had also become more flirtatious. The other day she had been busily vacuuming one afternoon in her lounge clothes, and he had made an offhand comment about how hot it was in their apartment now that the steam-heat had been turned on. She had agreed, saying that she was really sweating. Then she turned off the vacuum, an odd expression on her face. She had disappeared into the bedroom, reappearing moments later wearing nothing but her underwear. She had resumed her vacuuming without a word, but the sly smile on her face suggested that she was pleased Manolo had lost all interest in his newspaper.

The only thing she had refused to allow him to indulge in were his cigarettes. She said it was time for him to shake that nasty habit, and she had thrown all his cigarette cartons in the garbage. But without the old Natalya harping at him, he no longer felt an urgent need to light up. Except occasionally, when he woke up in the dead of night gripped by the thought that the old Natalya had returned. But each morning he was greeted at the breakfast table by a kind-hearted wife.

It occurred to him that perhaps she had multiple personalities, and that it was only a matter of time before the other Natalya resurfaced. But the new Natalya was so lovely and kind that he told himself this must be the real Natalya—the one he thought he had married three long years ago. The other Natalya was the impostor. Against his better instincts, he started warming to this lovely new version of his wife.

He found himself doing special little things for her, like buying her yellow tulips from the deli because they were her favorites. And he started picking his socks up off the floor each night—who knew that such a tiny little gesture would bring tears to her eyes. And he had insisted on cooking her dinner one night to repay her for all her recent efforts in the kitchen. Of course, his attempt at a Ukrainian "hunter's" stew had been completely inedible, but she had been touched by his effort, even as she begged him to steer clear of the kitchen.

And then one night this past week, as they were falling asleep in bed, she had asked him if he felt there was anything important missing from his life. This was the one subject Manolo had not yet been brave enough to tackle. The old Natalya had been very vocal about how much she despised children. But the new her proceeded to tell him about a young mother she had met standing in line at the drugstore that morning, and how very happy she had seemed cooing over her little newborn. Manolo looked into his wife's eyes, which were full of a hope and love that mirrored his own.

Manolo had always dreamed of having a large family. So this change of heart left him at a loss for words. All he could do in response was hug her tightly as he struggled to contain the emotions surging within him.

As Manolo looked back on the past week, he realized that it had been one of the happiest weeks of his life. He just needed to overcome the lingering doubts that were torment-ing him. But the scars left by the old Natalya were not so easily forgotten.

They were nearly done cleaning up the kitchen, his sister and Natalya chatting away the whole time like old friends. Manolo grabbed the last glistening plate from the rack with the damp towel he was holding. One second it was in his hands, and the next it had slipped through his fingers and crashed to the tile floor, where it shattered into a hundred pieces. Manolo froze as his eyes darted to Natalya. In the past broken dishes always triggered explosions of temper, and she would berate him endlessly for being so clumsy and useless. He realized instantly that he had unwittingly stumbled on the ultimate test for the new Natalya. This was the moment of truth, and Manolo broke out in a cold sweat.

"Oh, Manolo, what are we going to do with you?" chided a smiling Natalya. "Don't move. I'll grab the dustpan."

"Er . . . you're not mad?" he asked hesitantly.

"Of course not, my love. It's just a stupid dish."

"Are you sure? I mean—usually when I break something, you hit the roof."

"Oh, Manolo, that's so true. I don't know what was wrong with me. What a hateful witch I used to be. Do you think you will ever be able to forgive me?" She looked up at him with tears in her eyes.

"Of course, mi amor, that is all in the past." And as he said it, Manolo finally found himself believing it too. He embraced his lovely wife and exchanged a look with Maricela, who shrugged. *So that's it,* he thought. *This is my new life.* He resolved then and there to take a stroll down to the Botanica once a week, starting that very night, to light a green candle and pin a little thank-you note to Santa Muerte's robe—just to help keep the flame of love alive.

36. CONSTANCE

[one week later]

Her mother thought the whole thing was ridiculous. She kept asking Constance how long she had known him, politely at first, but with an increasingly abrasive tone. Constance's answer was always the same: just one week. But that's long enough for us.

Her mother had declined to make the trip, under the excuse that she couldn't afford New York City hotel prices. Instead, her uncle, who lived in New Jersey, had popped into town to represent her side of the family for the ceremony.

Roger's family had been equally perplexed, but at least *his* mother seemed intrigued by the possibility of finally getting her son out of the house.

Still, nearly everyone they knew had felt the need to let them know that it was totally nuts to jump into marriage so quickly. That's a good word for it, Constance always conceded, and then she would do her best to explain the upside to being nuts—such as the freedom to do whatever you liked without caring what people thought. This was met with puzzled frowns. Clearly the world wasn't ready to accept insanity as a lifestyle choice.

Not that any of that mattered. For the first time in years, she was deliriously happy.

Roger had brought up the idea on day three of their whirlwind romance. Beginning with their date at the bar, they had scarcely spent a free moment apart.

"Hey, Bunny," he'd said, "these have been the best three days of my life, and I don't want this to ever end. What do you say we pop down to city hall and tie the knot? That a crazy enough idea for you?"

The old Constance, who had been practical, down-to-earth, and cautious, would have run for the hills. But the new Constance had nothing in common with that sourpuss, and had agreed that it was a stupendous idea, adding that she saw no reason in the world to wait. Waiting was for wimps. Although she wasn't too keen on the City Hall part, as she was not fond of municipal buildings.

Roger had been crashing at her place, of course. Without pressuring her, he had made her see the need to drop off all her rabbits but one at the local shelter. It had been hard, but once it was over she had been hugely relieved. So it had been her, Roger, and her favorite bunny—Petunia— jammed into her little studio apartment for the past few days. Constance figured that if the wheels were going to come off the cart, it would have happened by now.

Not that she had a starry-eyed view of her husband to be.

Quite the contrary, she knew that Roger had questionable personal grooming habits, disturbing intestinal issues, and doubtful career prospects. No, her fiancé was a fixer-upper at best. But he was also sweet and attentive, and he deferred to her on all the important decisions, like what television programs to watch at night. She was sure that with a little coaching his trajectory in life could be greatly improved.

Constance had discovered he was perfectly capable of holding up his end of an intelligent conversation. He was surprisingly smart deep down. And she knew that if she chipped away at those doughy layers, she would eventually reveal his hidden talents to the world.

Even if she failed, he had the makings of a capable house-husband. He didn't seem to mind doing all the cleaning, shopping, and cooking, which were things she had very little patience for herself.

Warts and all, she was sure Roger would make a satis-factory life partner. Heck, she had a few rough edges of her own. He was prepared to overlook her sanity issues. He even pretended he was right there with her—mental health wise—even though he was clearly more of a wacky goofball, than a raving lunatic.

The wedding party gathered on the rooftop was small, consisting only of her uncle, Roger's mother, and a couple of friends each. Everybody was in costume. She had been very strict about that. No one in street clothes was allowed on the roof.

Constance was of course decked out in her rabbit cos-tume, with a delicate tiara pinned around her floppy pink ears. Roger was an upgraded Cloud Man—a purple suit with orange dyed cotton balls stuck to it, an orange bow tie, and steampunk goggles. Constance's two friends, who were both making a day trip into the city from suburbia, were both ostensibly sexy cats.

Roger's college roommate, Otto, the best man, was dressed as a lumberjack with a flannel shirt, a wool hat, and a fake ax. She liked Otto, whose only judgment about her, according to Roger, had been to proclaim her "a hottie." *Way to get on my good side forever, Otto.*

Roger's mother had reluctantly agreed to wear a Red Riding Hood cape they bought for her and was holding a small picnic basket that Constance had filled with confetti. Her uncle had done the bare minimum, showing up in a cowboy hat with a silver star pinned to his vest.

The officiant was wearing a showy werewolf costume. The photographer, a guy she knew from court, had showed up in a lackluster pirate costume. Thankfully, Otto had run over to the costume store and found a fake parrot to pin to his shoulder.

And lastly there was the band. She had knocked on Oliver's door and asked him if he could pull together some sort of musical setup for her rooftop wedding on short notice. He had been skeptical at first, claiming not to do weddings. But when she had offered to pay him and mentioned that costumes were mandatory, he had warmed up to the idea.

Oliver was in a convict getup, with black-and-white zebra scrubs and a ball and chain around his ankle. His black guitar was slung incongruously over his shoulder. He had talked two of his scruffy friends into joining him. One was a xylophone player dressed as a cop and the other a stand-up bass player in an astronaut costume. Her expectations had been very low. But so far they had pumped out very pleasing renditions of popular hits.

Anyone spying on their rooftop party—and a few faces had gathered in nearby windows—could not be blamed for thinking that Halloween had arrived early that year.

She had not asked for permission to use the roof for her wedding. Instead she had given her friend Julie, the maid of honor and ostensible sexy nurse, a hundred bucks, and instructed her to bribe anyone who tried to break up the party into looking the other way for twenty minutes. Once the ceremony was over, they could easily reconvene at a nearby bar for the celebration.

Standing up here, with the rumbling city all around them, Constance felt reassured that she had picked the right spot for their exchange of vows. Her lounge chair was still leaning against the wall right where she'd left it, and a few other abandoned junk items—an old grill, a broken TV antenna—were scattered about. She had told Roger not to bother tidying up.

But one thing that *was* missing was the water tower on the neighboring rooftop where she had glimpsed the alien creature. The fact that the tower itself was no longer there was slightly disturbing to her, as it made her question her insanity.

Roger had made an archway out of a battered old bed frame that he'd found in the trash, which they'd decorated with silver ribbon. Constance saw that the officiant had taken up her spot under it and was fanning herself with her notes. The guests were all sitting expectantly in a row of folding chairs. A plastic table over on the side had six bottles of tequila on it, along with some cut up limes in a jar, a dozen facedown shot glasses, and a chocolate ice-cream cake.

"Are you ready, honey?" Roger asked. She turned to face him and saw that he was looking at her giddily.

She smiled. Something she'd been doing a lot of lately. "I'm more than ready, darling. I'm raring to go."

"Me too! Let's do this. I'll go stand by the arch and give the signal to the band."

Constance looped her arm through her uncle's and stood waiting patiently until Oliver and his friends ripped into a badly mangled rendition of Wagner's "Ride of the Valkyries." She took a deep breath and started her walk up the makeshift aisle—grinning like a madwoman in her pink bunny suit.

37. OLLIE

[one week later]

⋮t was just getting dark when Ollie arrived at the Empress Café. The place was filling up with an early dinner crowd. Rhythmic Latin songs coursing through the speakers gave the café a lively vibe. He found both girls already sitting in a booth, a large plate of nachos placed on the table between them. Zara was drawing little cartoon faces on the chalkboard table surface, and Cassandra was happily shoveling tortilla chips loaded with beans and cheese into her mouth.

They exchanged cheerful hellos as he slid in next to Zara. He eyed the food hungrily, and Cassandra encouraged him to dig in. A blond waitress appeared to take his order. She scribbled down his choice of a falafel sandwich with fries on a small notepad, and promised to return soon with his beer.

"How's Pirate doing?" Cassandra asked him.

Ollie scraped some nachos onto a small plate with a fork.

"Oh, he's back to his usual self. Sleeping all day, eating his own weight in canned tuna, and pretending like he owns the place. He seems to have handled the shock of meeting an alien life-form a lot better than us."

"Yeah, everything still feels topsy-turvy to me," said Zara. "When I wake up every morning, I get this jolt when I remember what happened, and I think—is it really possible that a bizarre creature from another world was standing just a few feet away from us?"

The waitress popped up again, setting a bottle down in front of him. The two girls sat silently with frozen smiles on their faces as they waited for the server to move on. Hunching over the table, they continued their conversation in muted tones. "We'd better keep our voices down," said Cassandra. "We wouldn't want special agent whats-his-name knocking on our door, demanding to know why we can't keep our traps shut."

"At least the three of us can get together to talk about it," said Zara. "I think I would be going out of my mind if it had just been me."

"Hey, Cassandra," said Ollie. "Didn't you say the other night that your dad works for NASA or something? Do you think they picked up something on their scanners?"

"He is a scientist at SETI. But it doesn't work that way. They're not monitoring the atmosphere for alien incursions or anything. It's more about deep space listening and tedious data analysis of radio emissions. I wish I hadn't been sworn to secrecy because I'm dying to tell him about the whole thing. Although that fed dude had a point—my dad would never believe me."

"I keep wondering what happened to that catnapper lady," Zara said.

"My guess is that tin can is halfway to Jupiter by now," Ollie replied. "With that old bat along for the ride. Nothing she doesn't deserve."

"I'm not sure anyone deserves to be abducted by aliens," Zara chided.

"I'm with Ollie on this one," said Cassandra, slurping her soda. "She had it coming."

Minutes later their food arrived, and the conversation drifted to more mundane topics as they chowed down. Cassandra talked about her life on the audition circuit, and about a role in a commercial that she had just been passed over for. Ollie updated them on his job search, with some promising leads at a guitar store on Fourteenth.

"Listen. I can't hang out late tonight, guys," said Zara. "I need to catch up on sleep. My commute is killing me."

Cassandra brightened. "Well, you could always sleep over at my place."

"Really? That would be amazing!" Zara looked excited.

"Great, it's decided—you're staying over!" said Cassandra. "You can stay anytime, you know. Until I find an actual roommate."

"Yeah, about that." said Zara. "What would you think if I put my name down as a candidate?"

Ollie turned his head and stared at Zara. "Hold on a sec. Aren't you moving back to London in December?"

"As a matter of fact, I've been doing some thinking. There isn't really anything for me to move back for. I could easily find vet work here if I wanted and fly home for big holidays.

And my parents could pop over to see me whenever they like." She looked questioningly at Ollie. "What would you think if I extended my stay in New York for a year or two?"

Ollie couldn't believe she was thinking of staying. In his mind he saw his future opening up, and it was full of wonderful possibilities that hadn't existed moments ago. "Well, it would be fantastic news for the band," he said cautiously, still unsure how serious she was about this new plan. "I mean we'd never be able to find a singer half as good as you!"

"So is that all I am to you then? The singer in your band?" Zara skewered him with a look.

Ollie swallowed hard. This was it. She was putting him on the spot. And he knew that if he tried to play it cool, it would backfire on him. "Zara. I think you know how I feel about you. The only thing that's been holding me back was knowing that you were going to return home to London soon. But, Zara—if you stay, everything would be different. Please stay. I would be completely lost in New York without you. You know that."

Across the table from him, Cassandra let out a gasp and put her hand over her mouth. They both looked at Zara to see how she would respond.

"I do think you need me, Ollie. But what I didn't realize, not until the other day at least, when you very stupidly were about to climb onto an alien spaceship, was how much I need you too." She reached out and took his hand in hers. Her hand was small and warm and wonderful.

"Oh my god, look at you two love birds," said Cassandra, who was practically swooning. "Well that settles it. There's simply no way we're letting you move back to London. You're going to stay right here in New York and be my roommate and Ollie's girlfriend."

Ollie turned pink, and the two girls exchanged an "isn't-he-adorable look."

"I'll have to go over the math with my dad—he's the landlord—but ballpark I think we're talking around nine-fifty a month. Utilities included. Would that work?"

"I could definitely swing that." Zara grinned.

"Perfect!" said Cassandra. "And Ollie, you'll be right around the corner! The three of us can hang all the time! I'm so excited! I finally have real friends in New York."

"Four of us," said Ollie. "Don't forget about Pirate." He shoved the last corner of his sandwich into his mouth, and washed it down with a swig of beer. "I bet he could find his way to your place through the garden, no problem."

"Ollie!" said Zara crossly. "You aren't seriously thinking about letting Pirate outside again, are you?"

"Well . . . it's not like the city is crawling with catnappers and aliens. At least I hope it isn't."

"You are such a twit," Zara muttered, shaking her head.

"Pirate would be unhappy trapped indoors all the time," Ollie protested. "He's no ordinary cat."

"What do you mean?" asked Cassandra.

"Well, how many cats do you know who have escaped from a catnapper and befriended extraterrestrial life-forms?"

"When you put it like that I'd have to agree," said Cassandra. "He *is* a remarkable cat. I don't think I would keep him shut inside either."

"Look at you, siding with Ollie again," said Zara,

scrunching her nose at Cassandra. "I hope you don't plan to make a habit of that. But let's put that whole can of worms aside for now. When can I get a look at this two-bedroom pad of yours?"

"How does *now* sound?" Cassandra looked around at their empty plates. "I'll give you guys the grand tour."

"Ollie? You in for the tour?" Zara asked hopefully.

"I wouldn't miss it for the world.

38. AXZLEPROVA

[one week later]

Axzle coasted close to a huge gaseous planet, and then simultaneously boosted the vessel's jets while veering hard to port, using the oversized planet's gravity to slingshot their ship into deep space. It was his favorite maneuver, and the g-forces involved gave him a rush. Prova rolled her eyes at his unorthodox piloting.

Back on a straight trajectory, AxzleProva resumed the discussion of what to do with their human captive. The catch and release of the old woman had not gone according to plan. They had been chased out of the atmosphere by primitive human military air vehicles, and they had decided it would not be prudent to return to the planet's surface right away. Yet they weren't sure how much fuel they could spare hovering in the vicinity, waiting for things to cool down. Additionally they were concerned that after dropping off the old woman she would immediately go back to her violent ways. They had revived her long enough to attempt a cognitive reprogramming, but it had been an utter failure. The neural scanner had simply flashed red and popped up an error number. Looking up the error in the manual had revealed that reprogramming was out of the question with this older human female—her neural pathways were no longer flexible enough to be properly rerouted.

This had left them faced with a difficult dilemma. They could hang around, burning fuel, waiting for a propitious moment to return the woman to the Earth's surface, with her memory of the abduction intact. Or, they could take her with them and find some other way of unloading her on their way home. Axzle had been strongly in favor of option two. And Prova simply couldn't muster enough sympathy for the human female to convincingly claim that they had to release her on her home planet. Axzle had pointed out that she was nearing the end of her lifespan, and that it was doubtful anyone back on her home planet would miss her. He had emphasized that the woman would hold a strong grudge toward them and would be able to accurately describe them and their ship. If a credible rendering of them by an abductee ever made its way back to HQ, their careers would be over.

So in the end, they had simply returned the human female to the stasis chamber and set a course for home. Their frozen guest did not appear to be adapting well to the voyage. Prova had revived her twice and attempted to befriend her, letting her know they meant her no harm. But she had refused to speak to them through the interpretation device and had just glared at them menacingly. Recalling the vicious slash at Prova with the steel rod, they had taken no chances and quickly returned her to the chamber each time.

Finding a good spot to deposit her along the way had become AxzleProva's main topic of conversation. It had to be a planet or moon that had an oxygen atmosphere and a gravitational force similar to Earth's. That was the easy part. The planet also needed to be a real backwater, with no advanced indigenous or visiting life-forms to witness their clandestine operation. And lastly, Prova simply refused to drop her off anywhere inhospitable.

"Are you sure you don't want to just take her with us to the Galaxaga spaceport?" Axzle asked Prova once more. "We would be certain to find a black market taxidermist there who would take her off our hands for a decent sum, no questions asked."

Prova didn't dignify his suggestion with a response.

Axzle shrugged, giving up. "Well, let me do another deep search to see if there are any promising locations coming up in the next quadrant." He spent the next few hours tinkering with the research console. At last, his face lit up. "I found it! The third largest moon of planet Zarquak in the Omicron system. That is our spot."

Prova looked unconvinced. She had never heard of this moon.

They both huddled over the screen and examined Axzle's discovery. All the initial stats checked out: oxygen, gravity, and plentiful freshwater streams. But Prova quickly found fault. "It says here that the dominant life-form on this moon is a feline species known as the Puzzquo. They are carnivorous hunters." Prova pulled up an image on the screen of a fluffy tangerine-colored cat with large forward-facing eyes and knife-like teeth.

"Yes, but read the description my dear: they weigh about half as much as she does, and they only hunt the moon's abundant avian species. They live in colonies based around giant trees that dot their otherwise sandy planet. The cats hang from the branches of these enormous trees using their prehensile tails, and hunt by dropping down on any birds that pass beneath them. The birds are drawn close by the round fleshy pink fruit that falls from the tree, their only food source. It's a very simple ecosystem."

"Let me see," said Prova, tapping at the console. "This fruit seems similar in composition to an Earth's mango, so it should prove suitable sustenance for a human as well. But what will happen if she provokes the cats?"

"The dossier specifically states that the Puzzquo have never been known to harm any visitors. If provoked by out-siders, they simply turn around and spray their foul-smell-ing urine as a deterrent and are often joined in this by other members of their pack. The experience is not life-threatening, but it is rated as one of the least pleasant in this quadrant of the galaxy." Axzle grinned. "That explains why this moon rarely sees any visitors."

"That does sound vile," stated Prova. "But if this old woman learns to live in peace with the Puzzquo, then she will be fine. So yes, Axzle, I believe this moon is as good a place as any."

"It is quite idyllic, if you ask me," said Axzle, glancing over at their frozen captive. "She may well end up preferring her new home to her birth planet." Moments later he had input the new course, and the ship veered slightly downward and to starboard.

"That is certainly possible, my dear. But we will not be around to find out." Their antennae quivered happily, and Axzle leaned in to give Prova a quick kiss. Prova exchanged a conspiratorial look with her shell-mate as she casually reached over and flicked on the autopilot.

DELAS HERAS was born in Los Angeles, grew up in England and Spain, before settling in New York as a teenager. Delas has worked as a messenger, a genre fiction editor, an office temp, and most recently as a dance photographer. Delas lives in Manhattan with his wife and son.

Made in the USA
Las Vegas, NV
05 February 2021